Return of the Rupe

Rupe

(Ft Tiny Titch!)

Rachael Alonzo

This Book is Dedicated to

Ollie Fallon- Gervais @myleftfang the most beautiful kindest cat I know. Some other cats, dogs and humans may think it odd that I love you, what with me being a D.O.G but I find your eyes mesmerising, and your soul is warm and gentle. A great Philanthropist, you have done so much for the animals, you are a busy business cat, and one of a kind. Thank you for being my friend.

To my wonderful and kind PA Cathy Morton @CathyLaQuinta, whose commitment and expert eye has been greatly appreciated, without her help I think I would've gone barking mad ha.

I would also like to say that my book is supporting a wonderful charity @WetnoseAnimal, who do so much to rescue and save animals in need, you can visit their website www.wetnoseanimalaid.com to find out more and for every book sold I will donate 0.20p from my royalties to support the fight, so come on humans spread the word, tell your friends, relatives, neighbours, strangers even, buy this book and help save a life today.

And Finally thank you to all my followers, fans and family who support me and love me for who I am just a Fat Frog Sausage Dwarf Jack Russell dog, with a big heart.

Chapter 1 Life with a Bitch!

I've decided that as I'm now like a) famous, b) genius and c) expert in technology, I'm scrapping the diary (it was giving me cramp in my paws anyway) and I'm now entering the new age of Blogging, or in my case Dogging!! Erm, hang on ... might need to rephrase that as I've just looked it up and it can be RUDE... what kind of freaks are in this world.

Anyway, I'm now going to be doing a dog blog, so my ramblings will be recorded for all eternity. So back to it... oh and of course you now know Mad Bitch lives with us, she has joined my Twitter account (@Ruperttitch) and is sometimes allowed to tweet, but only occasionally, as it's all about MOI.

Talking of my crazy bitch "sister", who has been with us now for a month, she has today driven me to my patch! I swear to god she is seriously broken, she barks at everything, from a harmless leaf (stoopid!) to the turd-face postman, and my god she does not like him.

The other day he had to have a package signed for (just a copy of my first book, Diary of a Fat Jack Russell Aged 11 3/4, *cough!) ...Anyway, she managed to somehow escape, combat-style between Mummee's legs, and shot out of the front door. I was like UH OH! That poor postman didn't know what hit him, she was like a psycho Tasmanian devil (ha, remember the cartoon?). She went straight for his bag of post, and managed to attach herself to it and would not let go.... soooooo embarrassing! I was like FFS, Titch, get off the postman, you, crazy ass bitch! Jeez.

Mummee was mortified, she couldn't apologise enough to Mr Postie, and was very worried he would report her, but thankfully he saw the funny side and said he had met worse, and in fact had a dog like Titch at home, so I shouted, "well can't you take this mad bitch with you as well then?" ha ha ha.

My life now people is not my own, she steals my toys from me, gets in my comfy bed, is rude to all the other dogs on our walk, and she hates Douglas - when she sees him, her hackles rise and she immediately starts shouting "twat" at him continuously. I'm like OMG will you just stop, but then she bites me.

Some days she is nice, and so I get drawn in... she lets me wash her ears, and I love me an ear lick! I tried it once with Mummee, but got told off. I was like alright, alright, calm down, I haven't fucking tasered you! Titch on the other hand lets me do it, then bam – she snaps at me. I can't win; you girl dogs are so confusing. Anyway, at least I do have company now, even if she is a bit cuckoo, and since I've added to her to my Twitter account, we seem to get lots of attention. In fact, talking of Twitter, I haven't been on for a while, so off now to check the Twitterverse...

Well the Twitterverse has gone mental, I've got soooo much catching up to do, where do I start? Oh I know, I'll tweet my BF Stuffy, just tell her a quick joke to cheer her up...

"Why was the broom late? ... Because he over swept!" ha ha ha.

I shall tweet another one: what do you call a camel with no humps?

Humphrey! ha ha ha...

Just tweeted a pic of me looking suave, well I mean I don't look anything other, oh hang on, Mad Bitch is calling me, WHAAAATTTT, wait a minute will you, No, tweet your own picture, piss off... ouch, gerroff me, no! ...MUMMMEEEEEEE, tell her, TITCH stop biting your brother. HA in your face, what was that? You better not...

Well people she has only gone and pooped on the new rug, and is now blaming me, this is a disaster! I am really going to have to think of how I can get my own back, but for now a snooze fest is in order... OMG NOOOOOOO, get out of my comfy bed!

I am sick of this, I am now being subjected to Titch taunting me, she is standing on the sofa, whilst me, little old Fatso, is on the rug, as I cannot get up on the sofa these days without help. Titch is twerking at me, yes you heard t.w.e.r.k.i.n.g! WTF, oh for Christ's sake just get down will you, I am not indulging you today!

Ooo a new tweet from BF, wants to know how my get fit plan is going... As you are aware people, I have been trying to diet on and off all year, and not very successfully. Well I have just tweeted a little clip of me jumping for my squeaky sheepy toy, a toy that resembles a sheep and squeaks, well he used to, that was until I ripped his voice box out HA, that'll teach him, squeaking bastard.

BF says I look like a bouncing space hopper! I suppose I do, oh that reminds me of a tale from when I was younger and more agile. Mummee bought herself a bouncy thing for indoors, yes, I know people, you don't have to tell me the pitfalls of that! Anyway, I decided to get up on my own this one morning and had a mosey on down the stairs.

As I walked into the dining room area, I spied the bouncy thing and thought, ooo this looks fascinating, so took a run and jump and leapt on it, yes people you heard that right, stop sniggering. Anyway, there I was on bouncy thing and boy was it fun, that was until my brain switched to dig mode, yes this is a real thing, and I had an overwhelming urge to start digging, as I was convinced that under bouncy thing lay treasure.

Well, all I will say is that bouncy thing could not have been made very sturdily, as within minutes of me frantically digging for my treasure, I heard a ripping tearing sound and suddenly my head was poking through bouncy thing's bottom!

However, I then discovered I was stuck, and so started to panic. I tried barking but all that came out was a strangled whine, and I was now stress farting, phew weee.

Then a miracle happened - in walked Mummee, and I heard her shout, "what the hell, RUPERT, what have you done, Christ almighty, look this is ruined now, ruined!" I was like, fuck that, what about a little help here and getting me the hell out? Jeez.

Thankfully she released me from my bouncy trap hell, and I can tell you now, there was no treasure, and bouncy thing was a trickster and a twat. Mummee shouted at me, that was until Dad came down, saw what had happened and laughed his bollocks off, and said well if it hadn't been me that caused the hole, it was bound to have happened eventually with Mummee's arse jumping up and down on it! I don't know what he meant by that, but Mummee threw her slipper at him and they didn't speak for the day.

That was the end of bouncy thing, and I stayed snuggled by Dad all day, as Mummee was giving off a bad vibe.

Well I can hear Mad Bitch calling AGAIN, WHAAATTT NOW ? Just wait will you, well go find your bally, I'm busy, ok? Well I'm not telling you, am I. Jeez people, she is so high maintenance. Got to go - being called for walkies - so catch you later.

Just got back folks, and that was fun, haha! First off, I had green pooh, what's with that? I thought I had shit on a frog, but no, it was because of the green sticks Mummee gives me. Titch was horrified and ran off, but then, disaster - she bumped right into Ginger Bastard.

The last encounter she had with him didn't end well - he ended up swiping at her, and she was like all dramatic, as you broads are!

So, I had to quickly run to step in, as she might be a mad bitch, but she's MY mad bitch.

I ran, yes ran – ok stop laughing, in times of need I can summon up extra energy - so anyway, before you rudely interrupted, I RAN over to Ginger Bastard and whispered, "before you get any ideas about taunting my sister, just remember I know where you live!"

Pussy bastard soon backed off, and drama was averted. Off we trotted back home, and Titch stopped and kissed me! By kiss I mean she licked my nose, and I was so taken aback it caused a wheezing attack, which in turn caused Mummee to ask if I was ok, but then that set Mad Bitch off, with her yapping "what about me, what about me, what about me, what about me?" Oh, shut the fuck up!

So back home, and breakfast is served. I of course gobbled mine down in like thirty seconds flat, then tried to nudge Mad Bitch out the way of hers, but she has got smart to my ways - she did a low growl and said, *"back off Fatso, this here is mine"*. Alright, calm down, like I wanted it anyway!

Oooo Twitter alert, yes, I have alerts set up now, so I can check in on the action. Judge all you like, I know many of you people do this, so two words, piss and off. Interesting - a very gorgeous beautiful cat who has a very famous Dad (mentioning no names, but he is hilarious) has tweeted a pic of herself napping. I think I am going to follow this cat. Ordinarily I don't DO cats, but this feline is so sleek and soft-looking, and her eyes are mesmerising, they remind me of the twinkly lights on Christmas Tree – arrrggghhh, flashback!

So, I have followed the beautiful cat... I really hope one day she follows me back, how PAWsome would that be? Right, time to tweet my BF and tell her my news... hang on, I can hear Mad Bitch calling, again, I'm considering changing my name at this rate. Well, how can I help with that? She has lost her bally and it's gone under the sofa, I mean I ask you, she wants me to help - HELLO have you seen the size of my udderage? How the hell am I going to squeeze under the sofa?

Alright, I'm coming, listen, calm down, Mummee will retrieve it, ok? Breathe, that's it. Now shut up... OUCH, what was that for? OMG. I am leaving you to it.

Seriously people, this broad is broken... if she loses sight of her ball for one second she goes into meltdown, pacing round and round, muttering to herself, "Bally, Bally, Bally, Bally". It's like living in One Flew Over the

Cuckoo's Nest! Anyway, back to the Twitterverse...

Tweeted Stuffy and told her of my news, and, get this, she knows this cat, so I said, well get me an in then BF, but she said that was highly unlikely, as the cat called her Stuffed Bastard and was jealous of her! Oh well, I shall persist in my efforts to gain the attention of BC - short for Beauty Cat - until I break her down, haha. Hey, I am not a terrier for nothing you know, I am nothing short (yes, I am short) of being tenacious.

Talking of which, in my youth (when I was more able bodied!), I used to love to go on a reccy around the garden scouting for stinking vermin. I knew those bastards were there, just lurking in the undergrowth; my bionic nose would sniff them out... Oh hang on, WHAT NOW, FFS? I've told you before: when I am doing important stuff, you are not allowed to disturb me. Go ask Mummee, she will stroke you.

Sorry about that, just Titch being needy again... every day, my life with this bitch is one long round of checking she's ok, or being taunted by her, or calming her down, or trying to find Bally, and, lately, telling her she's a good dog. She must have had such a shit life before, maybe I shall get her to tell you the tale one day.

But, for now, back to me, me, me, me, and the stinking vermin story. There I was this one day pawtrolling the grounds, sniffing out them bastards, when I had the fright of my life! I actually leapt two feet in the air, I so did, OK, when out of the undergrowth hopped, yes hopped, this ugly brown lumpy thing.

At first, I thought it was a rat that had been at Chernobyl (HA!) but NO, it was something else. This thing started making such a weird sound - I was fascinated, it was like croaking - and then the thing got to leaping about, so naturally I tried to trap it with my paws, and OMG it was like sooooo slimy, YUK! I started to bark at it, and then I successfully managed to trap it in my mouth, but good god, it was like having a gooey ball of mucus in my mouth...eeeewwwww.

I tried barking to stop it wriggling around, but ended up nearly choking, so spat it out. Then, holding it with my paws, I started woofing loudly at it... Of course, this alerted Mummee, who has bat ears, (not literally) and she came running into the garden to see what all the fuss was about.

Well, you'd have thought I'd taken a cat hostage or something the way she went on.

She was shouting very loudly, LET IT GO! and I was like NO, finders- keepers! Then she came at me and tried to grab me, but I was way too fast for her back then, and skirted round her with said prize in my mouth.

I was running around the garden with this gooey, croaking thing in my mouth, and Mummee was hot on my tail! It was like a scene from Benny Hill, (cue music), however suddenly the weirdest thing happened - croaking slime ball somehow managed to free itself from my mouth and leapt to freedom.

Before I could catch him again, he had hopped under the bushes out of sight, and Mummee was shouting very angrily at me that I should never ever attack frogs. Ewww, is that what it was? Well alrighty then. But as a consolation, I later got to have Froggy No Eyes as a toy, (again people, this story is in my first book, download it now, what the fuck are you waiting for), so I had my very own frog. (When I got him of course he did have eyes…)

All this reminiscing has left me sleepy, I really need to snooze, so I am off now for a little lie down – will report back later.

Hell NOOOOOOOOOOOO, get out, get out, GET OUT! That's MY bed!

That told her, HA, now I'm circling, scratching, circling again, ooooommpf, and relax! Comfy bed has been claimed, now it's sleepy times.

Pssst, sssshhhhh [whispering]: it's me, Titch, do not tell him I have been writing in his ramblings, he will go mental, but I just must tell you, I've tweeted a video of him to BC (beautiful cat) and he was snoring very loudly, ha ha ha ha! That's for kicking me out of comfy bed.

Alright, people, that was some snooze fest, but I feel refreshed and alert, just going to check Twitter and see what's what...WTF, how the hell has that clip of me snoring gotten in there? OH, I think I know, TIIIIITTTTCCCHHHH, you're a mad bitch get here now, WHAT have you done? What do you mean, serves me right? It's my fucking bed. Oh God I am aghast.

Well, the shame and humiliation - BC is never going to follow me now, after seeing that! I looked like a giant bulging hippo, on my back, dognots on show, snoring for England, and it wasn't a gentle snore, NO, it was full-on grunting. Oh god, I tweeted BF, she nearly laughed her stuffing out! Well thanks. I'm going into hiding, and as for Mad Bitch - well, revenge is sweet.

Oh, that reminds me, talking of sweet...

Chapter 2   Yes, we have no Bananas

So, as you know, I have been on a get fit campaign, yes you do know, Christ almighty - SHUT UP Titch, stop laughing, sorry, how rude - anyway, during the campaign, Mummee made me try something different...

It was yellow and bendy and looked like a mutant to me, but no, Mummee convinced me it was nice, by eating some of this weird object herself. I gingerly took some into my mouth, and sucked it for a bit, but then spat it out. I just didn't like the texture, and it felt strange in my mouth. Of course, gob shite here came waltzing in and ate it off the floor, ewwww! *Well I thought it was nomtastic, yummy and sweet, I can't understand why you didn't like it, freak.* I'm the freak, wait until you hear what it was, then we shall see who the freak is.

I found out later that the offensive object was a banana, and supposedly is a nice healthy treat for dawgies. However, to be honest, I think hoomans are insane, as when I googled it, I discovered that it shares 90% of its DNA with you and so that would make you lot cannibals. I am NOT into that, yuk no, so my banana-eating days were short-lived, no bananas for me.

Titch, did you hear, it was called a banana, and shares its DNA with hoomans, so that would make you the freak ha ha, freak, freak, freak, OUCH, *stop calling me that now, I am neither a weirdo or a freak, and what kind of nonsense have you been reading on the internet again, you are such an idiot and will believe anything, I suppose you still think Elvis is alive.* OMG, ELVIS IS DEAD, when did this happen.........

Go back to your blog, for god's sake you really are stoopid !

I am so not stoopid, anyway, yes, we have no bananas, we have no bananas for me, YUK, however strawberries, well that is a different story altogether, and I loves me some of those, in fact we should get a good crop this year, nommm nomm nomm, sweet, juicy, lovely strawberries.

I think, some stretching is in order, and I am going to do my yoga, YES, I now do yoga, I attend class every Wednesday I shall have you know. Ok, downward facing dog first, then ooooommmmppppfff, just stretch myself out, *wriggling, aww that's better, I feel all calm and lovely, just arch my back, now time to call mad bitch, revenge is sweet........ Oi Titch, come here, I have something for you, you need to come and see.

What is it, what is it, what is it? Let me see, let me see, let me see! Just check to see if I have anything stuck to my fur for me please, PPPFFFFTTTTT HA HA HA HA HA, *Ewwww that is disgusting, RUPERT you dirty stinking foul cretin, gerroff me! MUUUUMMMMM, Rupert has farted right in my face and it stinks bad. Just you wait.*

Ha, that was for stealing my comfy bed earlier, let that be a lesson to you, comfy bed is mine. Do you know what folks, too much excitement for one day, I feel a snooze coming on, so I'll catch up with you later off to claim comfy bed so, SSSHHHHH dog snoozing.

*whispering, it's me Titch, whilst fatso is sleeping, I think I shall tweet his BF and tell her what he's really like, see what she says then. Ok this is what I have put,

Hey Stuffy Stuffington or whatever your name is, I bet you didn't know your BF fatso likes to fart in my face, he is a stinking bag of wind.

Hehe, see what she says later, for now I think I might join tortoise and have a little nap myself, I shall see if there is any room in comfy bed.

Oi, when did you squeeze yourself in comfy bed, I thought it was one of my toys, I was lying on, come on move out of the way, I need to check Twitter, but first I need a treat, my sugars are low after that nap......

Are you having a giraffe, your sugars are low, jeez fatso, you need to stop with the treats, that's why you sway when you walk, if I were you, I would think twice, before finding Mum, and asking for a treat, can't you resist.

Let me make something clear, 1. I am not you, 2. Keep your nose out, 3. No I can't resist and 4. I so do not sway when I walk RUDE.

Nommm nommm, Nomm nomm,, want some mad bitch, NO, ok then more for me, nom nomm nomm. Love the body you are in, there is too much pressure in this world on what you should look like, I like my shape, round, who doesn't like round, balls are round, *did you just say BALL, where, show me,* FFS get your nose out, like I was saying pizza is round, donuts are round, what is not to love about round, so fuck it, don't like me, keep walking pal. Talking of walks, come on Titch we need to go for ours.

Just got back, that was by far the most awkward yet, we bumped into stinky-breath Henry, you remember him? Oh well, if not, he's got an arse the size of the backend of a bus, and he's like a cross between a bull and a dog, poor sod, but his breath is the worst - it's like stinking camel shit. I have the decency to stand well back and not comment on it, but Mad Bitch here, well she has no tact or diplomacy whatsoever.

She walked up to him today, right in his face, and says, *"here Henry, anyone ever tell you, your breath is sooooooo bad you could strip paint with it?"* MY god I thought he was going to keel over, he looked mortified! Then he put his paw to his mouth, breathed on it, and smelt it, and to be fair he said, "well that is the first time I've noticed" (seriously mate?). Anyway, he said he suffered with his breathing as his face was so mushed up and perhaps this caused the stink... I said NO pal, more like you get given shit to eat and it's lingering on your breath.

That wasn't the worst of it... We passed Douglas, same shit different day, and then she spotted Frankfurter (Klaus the sausage dog). Oh, Jesus Christ, I thought, let the ground swallow me up... Off she went, bark, bark, bark, bark, then chased after him on her bungee, shouting, *"Flachwichser!"* Erm firstly I didn't know she knew German, and secondly, how insulting, calling him a flat wanker! Haha, good job he didn't hear her.

So that was the walk, very embarrassing. Mad Bitch is now sitting in the lounge keeping a lookout for the postman, who she knows will descend upon us very soon! Me I am chomping on my breakfast, oooo, and I am in luck, Titch has left some of hers, so no waste here, nomm nomm nommm... Oh piss off, I can hear you all judging me, talk to the paw.

Better check Twitter and see what's going down, need to do my daily tweet to BC and get her attention somehow. Ooo, I know, I shall send her a little ditty...

Well this is what I tweeted: "Here I am furry and soft, Rupert's my name, wanting you is my game, give me a wink with your eyes so blue, Oh, wait a minute I think I need a pooh."

If that doesn't do it, I don't know what will! She does have an awful lot of admirers, and I am a DOG, but you never know - my persistence may one day pay off.

Tweeted Stuffy my BF and asked what she had been up to, she first came back with a picture of gas mask on her face, weird, I tweeted back asking WTF? and get this, Titch the crafty cow, only went and sent a tweet grassing me up saying I farted in her face, now BF thinks I am a gross gas bag, I did go on to explain why, but BF said, I should share, and farting is just so uncouth.

I said did she never fart, but apparently not, she tried to release some trapped wind once, after being stuck in a windy alley, but it knocked her sideways, and lay like that for days, so now she avoids getting caught in draughty areas. Oops, I said I would try and be more of a gent from now on!

I asked her if she had any other news, and get this, she and Mr Chicken are well and truly over, he's gone to work at the Pink Flamingo as a drag act, named himself Miss HEN - RIETTA! For those of you who don't know, Mr Chicken was her first love, however he couldn't decide if he liked Cocks or not, he came out of the closest, but went back in, it was like the hoky-poky for a while!

Anyway, it seems she now has a new love interest, some sailor cat - I have warned her about him, and said that he might have a puss in every port... we shall see how it turns out, but for now I am happy for my BF - she deserves love, we all do. I am lucky, but some poor dawgies never find their forever home. That makes me sad, but at least we saved one, even if I didn't want the mad bitch at first.

And, let me tell you, that first week was hell! Oh, hang on...now there's somebody at the door, Mumme is shouting this loudly, like I can answer it, well, I can't, slight height and thumb issues! DUH also I'm a dog, in case you have forgot. *Who is it Rupert, do I need to do my manic bark,* let me go see, ooooo it's my Aunty Suzie Tongue, ha ha. I don't think she knows Mummee calls her that, but it's because she talks, and talks and talks forever!

Calm down TITCH, she's friend not foe, yes, she's come to see YOU, god knows why though, as you're a mental case. You've only been here a fucking month and already you are like lady muck, prancing around and accepting visitors. I didn't get this attention,

PAH! Well you had better be on your best behaviour, ok?

Aunty Suzie, Aunty Suzie, Aunty Suzie, it's me Rupert, do you have any treats? What, no? Well talk to the paw, selfish twat. OMG, Mad Bitch has pissed herself, Aunty only bent down to stroke her and she's pissed all over the floor, dirty cow. I can just imagine if I'd done that... I tried once years ago, they had just bought a new chair, and I started sniffing the leg of it, and thought, hmmmm, need my scent on that, so cocked my little stump and was just about to relieve myself, when Mummee shouted so loudly at me, I almost passed out like one of those goats, ha ha.

Anyway back to Aunty, she's only come to see Mad Bitch, so I'm off for a snooze. Wake me for treats only, ok.

Psst it's me TITCH, ssshh, ok? I've had soooo much fuss from this Aunty person - she even sneaked me a treat! Don't you tell Fatso, who by the way is still snoozing his fat head off, he sounds like a hog, hehe... Well got to go, our secret ok?

Ppppfft, oh, excusez-moi, a bit windy today, good job nobody was around to hear and smell that baby what with me trying to be more of a gentleman, can only assume it's the lack of attention... anyway I think Aunty Suzie Tongue has gone, so I shall check Twitter.

Talking of Twitter and my account, *ERM * coughs, I think you mean OUR account fatso,* It was mine to begin with, and I am sick of you sneaking on and tweeting absurd stuff about me, so I am going to put a password on and I'm not telling you, no siree, piss off, so whinge and cry all you like, if you want to tweet you have to ask me now.

Dammit, I need to figure out that password, I bet it's "Mummee", as he's such a mummee's boy. I shall try it when he's not around...

Well folks, I have checked the Twitterverse, not a lot happening, so I have tweeted another little ditty of mine, it went like this: "I'm a little Fatso short and stout, here's my tail and here's my snout. Lift me up... if you can..." HAHA!

Everyone found that funny, and they want more. I shall have to use my ingenuity and come up with a different one tomorrow. Tweeted BC a picture of me looking suave as ever! I hope she likes it, I mean what's not to love about me, cute button nose, big mesmerising eyes, soft fur, cuddly... haha, sounds like one of them old dating adverts you hoomans used to place in the paper looking for love. Now you're all about Tinder, and looking for a hook-up or some such nonsense.

Instead of having your head looking down at your phones, how's about looking up for a change and holding an actual real conversation, DUH.... Jeez, good job us furry warriors don't have to swipe left or right, well Ginger Bastard would like that, but no, it would be a dating disaster. Swipe right, turn up expecting a Jack Russell who described herself as tri-colour, looking for fun with balls, a bit OCD.

But then, get to the park, and there's like ten of them bitches all barking, and running around with balls, so how the fuck am I supposed to spot "The One"? NAH, I think I shall stick to good old-fashioned arse sniffing, and then a lick of the face, if I likey. You hoomans should try it! HAHA, imagine walking into a bar, or wherever you go these days, then sniff an arse, lick a face, order a drink, take a selfie, job done.

Well, Nanny Hammy and Granddad Potato once said that in their day, it was a lot more civilised, and not a bit like this nonsense now. Good God, Nanny said if she had to use a dating app now, it would be carnage, I mean how on earth would she know if they had their own fucking teeth, for starters? I was laughing so hard at that, I had a wheezing attack. Poor Nanny thought it was because I was upset she might leave Granddad!

Talking of Nanny Hammy and Granddad Potato, they haven't been round all week... I hope to god they are ok, I shall go and check with Mummee, maybe Mad Bitch scared them off. She can go over the top, and gives people a headache. Back soon…

Soooooo, I have just found Mummee, hang on… WTF, why do you always pester me when I am busy? NO, I haven't seen Bally, have you left him outside? Well, GO AND LOOK, idiot…I can't come and help you look, no, FFS… back in a mo, people… I'm going to help her look, otherwise my life will be made a misery, fact!

Ssshhhhh,it's me Titch, I have quickly sneaked back in, whilst Fatso is out looking for my bally, good plan or what? He has forgotten to put the password on, so HA, who's the idiot now? So Nanny Hammy and Granddad Potato will be here later - I know this because Mummee said they were coming to see ME ME ME, as I am so beautiful.

Fatso hasn't been told as he will sulk, so don't tell him... SHHIIIIT, he's coming ... Quick...

Right here is your fucking BALLY, now piss off and leave me will you, also do you know when Nanny and Granddad are coming? WHAT, today? Well why the fuck wasn't I told? OMG my life sucks, you have stolen the limelight again...

Don't talk to me... I am going to my bed...

OH Rupeee, Nanny Hammy is here, where's my favourite little boy then, come on I have a treat for you! PAH you are only trying to appease me before you shower all your affections on Mad Bitch here, who by the way has not shut up barking since they arrived, SHUT UP will you? FFS, you don't have to bark for attention anymore.

Nomm nommmm nommmmm, not bad Nanny, a very tasty treat, pulled out all the stops, haven't you? Oh god, listen to 'em, cooing over her, anyone would think she's like a royal baby or something. I'm going to tweet BF and get some fuss from her.

Well, my life sucks. BF was unsympathetic, saying I should be kinder to Titch, especially after what happened to her, and besides kindness is magic...well, perhaps she is right, in fact I might even get Titch to tell you her story. Better get your hankies, it's sad - even caused a lump in my throat, oh hang on, that was a piece of denta- stick that got stuck, ha.

Well, I can hear Mummee calling me, as Nanny and Granddad are going now. Oh right, can't even be bothered to stay and fuss over Rupert, well screw you, I'm freezing 'em out. WHAT, Titch? Yes, yes, Nanny and Granddad are very loving, blah blah blah, whatever. Oi Mad Bitch, I will need you to tell your story for my dog blog, so when you've finished being a princess, do you think you could spare me some of your precious time? What do you mean, maybe? NO, I am not giving you a regal name. WTF, I am NOT calling you that, don't be ridiculous, how on earth can anyone call you Princess Consuela Bananarama Ninny Nanny Noo Noo? NO, fuck off, now come and tell me your story.

Chapter 3   Heartbreak

Hi, it's me Titch, I am actually being allowed to write in his stoopid dog- blog... IT'S NOT STUPID! *Alright, alright, calm down. If you are going to stand over me, then at least shut up, so I can concentrate.*

Folks, you will have to bear with me, as usually I am not very social and find it difficult to express myself without SHOUTING, oops sorry, and I have OCD tendencies, in fact where is Bally, Bally, Bally, Bally? YOU ARE SITTING ON IT, idiot! *Oh, shut up, Fatso, will you leave me now so I can type?* OK, just don't get distracted.

This is my story…

I am the same breed as Rupert, my new brother! This fact is hilarious, as I can tell you now, I am neither a smelly boy nor a FATSO like him, in fact I am melt-your-heart pretty, check me out on @Ruperttitch.

However, I do have a personality problem, and am probably classed as hypersensitive, or mad, as Rupert calls me… not mad in the true sense of the word i.e. lost my marbles, but I am a little paranoid, skittish and afraid of everything and certain people, mainly men – oh, and postal persons!

You can understand why he calls me "Mad Bitch", as I am female, and that's what girl dogs get called - I know, not very nice. Thankfully Rupert / Fatso doesn't have urges, well at least I thought he didn't.

When I first arrived here, it was quite daunting and very, very scary. Fatso here did nothing to help the situation... WELL YOU DIDN'T! Shut up and let me tell the tale. Day three was awful, and after I tell you about the offending situation, we shall never speak of it again.

Rupert tried to mount me, yes you heard right, laugh all you like, but for me it was horrific, like being savaged by a giant fat furry tortoise! Not only that, Rupert is a) shorter *than me, being the dwarf bastard he is, b) FAT and c) eeewww, he was going to be my brother!*

The fat little bastard couldn't even get his balance after trying to jump on me, so he fell over and rolled on to his back, udders flopping everywhere. HEY, I AM HERE YOU KNOW! *Anyway, as I was saying, there he was, little stumpy legs in the air, and so I took my chance. I pinned him down, and whispered in his ear, "you try that again EVER, and I will not only bite your dingle dangle off, I shall take your place as numero- uno, do we understand each other?" After that he was like putty in my hands.* I WAS SO NOT! *Oh, shut up.*

Like I say, folks, very offensive, and never to be raised again. So back to me, yes, I can be high maintenance, yes I sometimes have weeing accidents, but I am extremely loving, and all I ever wanted was to be loved back, and not endure torture like I had to before I was saved by my new Mum and Dad, who I love so very much…

TIIIITTTCHHHH come quick, I see a mousey outside, I swear, quick, need backup. *Bloody hell, I am trying to type my story like you have asked me to do.* YES, I KNOW, BUT MOUSEY…

I am back, it wasn't a mousey but a sodding leaf. I said he needs to get his eyes tested, but he didn't like that, as he reckons his eyes are bionic. Yeah, whatever, at least I know the difference between a mouse and a leaf, but still it was fun and I haven't had a lot of that in my life… I shall continue with my story.

When I was a young pup, I thought my life was going to be full of fun, laughter, love and warmth. It couldn't have been more different. I was subjected to hours of being shouted at, by a human who wasn't even my Dad, and I was forced to live in squalor, in a tiny cage, and sometimes, shamefully, I even had to eat my own pooh! That was not my choice but I had to do it just to survive… some days I would be so hungry, as he would not leave me any food, and my stomach would rumble, it was distressing and painful. Then came the terrifying ordeal, which has scarred me for life…. What Rupert? No, I haven't finished, you said for me to tell my story, so I am… Well, be patient, go and have a snooze, ok.

Bloody Fatso, sorry, where was I? Oh yes, one day I was trying to get warm by crouching under some old newspapers, when suddenly that bastard came in and grabbed me by the scruff of my neck, and yanked me out from under them, and I was so frightened.

He carried me to this damp, smelly, cold room next door, and all the while I was thinking, what's he going to do with me? I was yelping and whimpering, but this made him angry – he shouted at me to quieten down, then he dumped me on this hard, rough table.

This next part really does haunt me… Before I knew what was happening, a very tight object was wrapped around my tail, and I cannot tell you the pain I felt. This thing was squeezing so tight, I thought surely, he is not going to leave it like that, but he did, and what is worse, it got even tighter. I now know it was a rubber band, used illegally to dock the tails of our breed. Thankfully they don't do this barbaric act any more.

The pain was so intense I started howling, but he smacked me on my nose, and I was so terrified that I shut up. But all I could think about was surely, I need my tail, how will I *greet other doggies, show happiness, joy, or love? This bastard obviously didn't care about that. Soon I was roughly carried back to my cage, and then he left.*

I had to endure this pain for a few more days... I tried to sleep, but it was unbearable. I had no food, I was cold, and I started to shiver; I couldn't feel my tail anymore, and to my horror, I realised it had become infected. I was close to death. When the bastard returned, he realised this, so he grabbed hold of me, drove me somewhere, and dumped me, like a sack of rubbish.

It turned out to be my salvation, as some kind people found me in the nick of time, and rushed me to the emergency vets, where they had to perform life-saving surgery. It resulted in me losing most of my tail, as they had to amputate a lot of it, and now I am left with what looks like a tiny chipolata sausage. I can still wag it, just about, and I have gotten used to not having a tail. I was just so grateful to the vets who saved me.

Of course, they couldn't find the bastard who did this to me, but I know he's out there somewhere... I can only hope that one day he gets his comeuppance.

After I spent a week at the vets, and was healing nicely, they unfortunately had to send me to the local dogs' home for rehoming. I am afraid I didn't fare very well in there, and it was some time that I stayed, as everyone who saw me thought I looked odd without a tail, and of course I hadn't been socialised as I was taken from my Mummee too early, so I got bypassed for cuter-looking dogs.

All in all, I was in that place for a year, then a miracle happened, and the rest, as they say, is history. My new Mum and Dad, and of course Fatso Rupert, fell in love with me, well maybe Rupert didn't at first, but I know secretly he loves me now, and I feel safe and loved for the very first time in my life.

So, folks, that's my story, but it has a happy ending, and my life now is all about teasing Fatso, barking at the postie, chasing bally, sleeping in a nice soft bed, food when I want it and so much love. It's bliss... Oh alright I have finished, I shall hand you back to Rupert... here, have your stoopid dog blog back...

Jeez, I thought she was going to ramble on forever, I only said tell 'em what happened, not write your fucking biography... Owwww! alright, I am sorry, go and find bally. What did I tell you people, sad or what, and I don't think that's all, but she gets too upset talking about it, maybe she will fill us in, later.

Just checked Twitter and tweeted BF, she said she had a message from Miss Hen-Rietta, as he is now calling himself. He said that he hoped they could still be friends and would she go to his show... I said that might be fun, what does he sing? She said, "I am what I am", haha.

I tweeted a pic of me to BC and said how stunningly beautiful she looked today; she tweeted back and said I looked like a fat idiot! I asked Stuffy what else I could do, but she said nothing - BC has so many admirers it would be a miracle if she ever fell for a D.O.G. Oh well, I will not give up - they don't call me tenacious for nothing.

Hmm, I haven't heard from my PA in a while, maybe she has left the country or something... Oh yes, sorry I forgot to mention

I have a PA now, she corrects the grammar and spelling in my tweets and reminds me about my appointments; she is also the editor of my books, in fact she is editing this one right now! She is kind, funny, smart and beautiful... HEY, GET OUT OF HERE PA! This book is crowded enough with Titch barging in, I don't need you adding your comments as well! I will have to speak to Stuffy (she is Stuffy's PA as well) about giving PA a written warning. She is a good PA, but can be insubordinate at times.

Well back to Twitter, I now have, OUCH! sorry, WE now have over 400 followers, which is quite remarkable! Must be my cuteness... I beg your pardon, well how can it be you, and your pretty face? You only joined a month or so ago. Oh whatever, anyway I can hear our Mummee calling us, must be time for a walk, so come on Mad Bitch, let's go and terrorise the neighbourhood.

Chapter 4   Double Trouble

I cannot believe it, that walk was awesome. We have decided to team up, and we realised that together we can cause double trouble!

Ginger Bastard was shaking in his fur this morning. Oh, for those of you who don't know who Ginger Bastard is, he's a ninja mouse-killing cat who likes to taunt me on my walks... Oh and one time he got trapped in a shed for a few days... NOTHING to do with me, OK...

Titch was brilliant, she can raise her hackles up high on her back, and when we came across Douglas the idiot, she caught him unawares and started barking at him first, shouting "*dumbo, dumbo, dumbo!*" Haha, this is brilliant.

She abused Frankfurter the sausage dog again. I mean last time was bad enough, calling him flat wanker - well today she shouted "*Schlappschwanz*", which means, literally, "weak dick", OMG! I asked her how she knew so much German, and she said it was from when she was in the kennel for a year. She was housed next to a German Shepherd - NO not a shepherd who was German, fools, a dog! - and he taught her.

I said I thought it was brilliant that she was bilingual, and could she teach me, but she said no, as the saying is true that you can't teach an old dog, new tricks, plus I am an idiot. Excuse me, I said, my IQ is like 59, so fuck off, and anyway I know Italian ("spaghetti" and "capiche"), so in your face, Mad Bitch.

Sometimes we banter back and forth, but in the main now we are united, and on our walks, we stick together.

Back now and eaten breakfast. Titch is getting used to it and realises if she doesn't eat all of hers I will, and so gobbles it down. I think a snooze is in order now, all that activity on the walk has left me sleepy. FFS what now, I was just going for a snooze, what do you mean if I snooze I lose, lose what exactly? NO WAY, YOU GET OUT OF MY PATCH NOOOOOWWWWWWWW.

That is bang out of order, and NOT what we agreed. The patch is mine! I tell you now, people, the truce is off. That bitch has been in my patch and dug out all my trophies.

Oh yes, I have a patch in the garden that I call my serial killer patch, and it is where I bury items I have stolen. Most recently, I buried a glove I stole from Nanny, and, just the other day, I pinched a pair of Dad's pants from the laundry and ran off with them. They are now buried in my patch, well they were until cow bag here went and dug everything out.

You put them all back now, or else! What do you mean, or else what? I shall hide your stupid bally, HA that's got you, look at your face now! Bally has gone, I have chewed him up, GERROFF me, arrgggghhhhhh! MUMMMEEE, MUMMMEEE...

What is going on out here? Titch, get off your brother, stop biting his ears. Rupert, look at the state of this garden, why on earth have you dug a hole, and what are all these items? Why have you got your Dad's pants, and is that Nanny's glove? You, naughty boy.

I HATE YOU, no gerroff me, I am not talking to you now ever.

I cannot tell you, people, the anger I am feeling right now. Firstly, Mad Bitch feigned ignorance and completely denied any knowledge of the hole, which may I add SHE MADE BIGGER! Secondly, she bit me, and thirdly Mummee has taken my items, filled the hole in, and said I am a naughty boy.

Could this day get any worse? I am depressed beyond belief. That was my patch, my bit of secret pleasure, and now it's ruined. I don't want to talk about it anymore, leave me alone.

I have tweeted Stuffy, my BF, and told her what happened. She said I should've pushed Titch in the patch, haha yes, I would have if she hadn't been pinning me down. (I didn't tell BF that bit, don't want to look like a complete twat.)

Tweeted BC, told her again her beauty knows no bounds, all she said was "I know" - a very modest cat, she is! NO, tweet your own picture, after what you have done you're lucky you are still on the account. Oh sod it, here, happy now?

I have had to tweet a pic of her, looking all pretty and stupid, well you are... OMG already it's had 38 likes. Jesus Christ, I am going to my bed, and she better not be in it...

Awww bliss, some quiet time, just me, my snuggly bed and ARRRggghhh - WTF, what is she barking at now? Oh my god, it's bin day, so the bin men are here outside, and she is going proper mental. This I must see.

Haha, you are not going to believe this, she is leaping from sofa to sofa, and ripping all the cushions! Mummee is going to go ape when she sees her. I better intervene. Oi Titch, calm down, it's only the bin men, they come once a week for the rubbish. Stop barking, otherwise Mummee will come in and see what you have done, which may I add is rather extreme. WHAT? I cannot understand you through your bally. Oh yes, I forgot to add people, all the time she has been leaping around she has had Bally in her mouth. Haha, she looks like them weirdos I saw once on the internet who are into strange S & M shit, what is it with your hoomans? p.s. I wasn't looking at doggy porn...

Uh oh, Mummee is coming. What the hell, what have you done to my bloody cushions? Rupert, was this you? ERM NO, it fucking wasn't me, it was Mad Bitch here, saw the bin men and went bat shit crazy. For goodness sake, can't have anything nice with you... What do you mean, with me? When have I EVER ragged the cushions? Get out, the pair of you, go on...

Titch, you have gotten us into trouble now, thanks a lot, what is wrong with you? Oh, well now I understand. She said she thought one of the bin men was the bastard who tortured her, and so it sent her into a blind panic. I understand, but you must realise that you are safe now, ok? Go and lie in comfy bed, yes, I will let you.

Well, as I am awake might as well hit Twitter, see what's going down... Ooo BF has tweeted me, and said that her new love interest is coming back from sea and would like to go on a date. I have told her to go somewhere safe, text me, and do NOT invite him back, he could be a doorstop killer! She wasn't impressed with that last bit. Well, it's for her own safety...

Lots of tweets from animal shelters, with poor furry warriors looking for homes... I must say I am lucky, these poor souls have no one - it's a cruel world you hoomans have created. If everyone had the same ethics as us dogs, the world would be a better place.

Tweeted BC a picture of me and her in a hot air balloon and said I could take her to the stars, but all I got back was a firm NO. What is it with this cat, she thinks she is funny... well her Dad is hilarious, Mummee told me about him, said his humour is very real and he pulls no punches, whatever that means, so I watched a clip of him on the You tube. He was in a show called The Office, and yes, I admit he is a funny man. He was doing a silly dance, and it made my udders bounce through chuckling. I may see if I can follow him, I forgot his name though, must remember to ask Mummee.

OOO, I can smell toast, I am sure of it... back in one minute, well maybe ten, depends on what is on offer....

Nommmmmm nommmmmmmmm nommm, had me some toast, and even shared it with Titch, who has calmed down somewhat. We are going to play outside later, with Bally and a new toy I have, Mr Pheasant Bastard. He was sent to me by one of my adoring fans, Vicki is her name and following me is her game, she is a very pretty lady, wit- woo.

I can hear Mummee shouting, hang on... Oh, someone is at the door? Well answer it then, why are you telling me? She has started doing this, like I can reach up and answer it, how strange would that be? I'd be like, through the letterbox, "who is it, what do you want, nobody is home, fuck off!" Ha ha, that would be brilliant, nobody would ever come again.

Oh, I get it now, she's warning me, as when the knocker goes, Titch is going to go into a frenzy, AGAIN. Here we go... in 3... 2... 1... *WOOF, WOOF, WOOF, WOOF, WOOF, WOOF, WOOF, WOOF, WOOF, WOOF, ALERT, ALERT, ALERT, DOOR, DOOR, DOOR!* Yes alright, we get the message, there is some twat at the door. I wonder who it is.

Ha, well this is going to be interesting, it's that man friend of Dad's, the one who smells of snakes, cheese and onion, and oil. He hasn't seen Titch before, and she does not like strange men.

Mummee is warning him. I can hear her saying, she was a rescue, and yes please be kind, perhaps give her a treat... Hang on,

BACK THE FUCK UP... give her a treat? Did I just hear, right? How come, when people came to the house BMB (that's Before Mad Bitch, HA, like AD or BC), I was never offered treats? Oh, wait hang on, that's not technically true, as every Monday Nanny used to come and bring me a treat.

In fact, why doesn't Nanny come now, on a Monday, what has happened? Oh, I know, it's because of Titch, she ruined it. Nanny said that for the first couple of months, she would leave her to settle in and get a routine, then would start coming again. Well I hope she stockpiled food and biscuits, as when she came here she ate us out of house and home.

For those of you who are not aware, Nanny Hammy eats biscuits all the time, and when she comes to our house, shoves them in like there is no tomorrow! [pssst don't tell her I said this though ok.]

Dad is talking to the snake man now in the kitchen, and Titch is yapping at his feet, shouting, *"look at my bally, look at my bally, look at my bally, look at my bally!"* He doesn't fucking, care about your goddam bally, shut up will you? Ouch! I thought you and I were going to be nice to each other, and all you've done is cause trouble for me, yeah well you better be sorry.

SHIT, what was that bang? Oh my god, Titch has hidden under the table, and I must admit I've nearly crapped myself, in fact I have stress farted, oops, ha ha. Dad is looking suitably disgusted at the smell, well sorry, but that scared me. What the hell was it? Apparently, it was the farmer - he was letting off a bird-scaring gun, as he gets lots of rooks and pigeon bastards in his field, not far from where we live. Well he could've posted a warning, twat. I nearly jumped out of my fur.

In fact, it reminded me of a time when I was a young pup, and it was before Mummee and Dad let me in big bed... they made a bed up for me in the kitchen, which at the time was freeze your bollocks off cold. It was in the old house, and the kitchen was an add-on!

The stupid previous owners had made a cat flap in the back door, but get this, they had also made another one in the internal kitchen door that led to the lounge. I mean I ask you, how fucking stupid can you get? How about just getting off your fat arses and letting the cat in? (Good job it didn't live there when we moved in... I can just imagine it, the cat creeps in in the middle of the night, and there's me, ha! I don't know who would've been more shocked.)

Anyway, these stupid cat flaps caused a draft, and rather than Mummee and Dad buying a new door (well Mummee would have, but tight arse Dad said no, as we were only renting) (did I mention my Dad is a skinflint?), they decided to cover it with newspaper!

So, there I was, shivering in my basket under a blanket, thinking this is shit, what kind of torture is this? In fact, I think I can understand how Titch felt... OH HANG ON, here she is poking in – WHAT? Ok, ok, I have no idea how it was for you - calm down, it wasn't fucking Schindler's List... Owwwwww, gerroff me.

Where's your bally? Ha, off she goes, gone to pester snake mechanic man who is still here, worse than Suzy Tongue he is for rabbiting on! So, I shall continue the tale... Like I was saying, I had to sleep downstairs when Mummee first brought me home, and I hated it, so much so that I used to cry all night, whimpering at the little cat flap that was now covered in newspaper. I ask you, how tight is that? Mummee was horrified, and said that Dad was so tight his shoes squeaked when he walked... I have never heard him squeak, to be honest, so I think Mummee is making up stories again.

So, this one night, it was howling with wind and rain, and a storm was brewing outside. I was trembling in my bed, and barking as loud as I could, but nobody could hear me above the storm, either that or the bastards were stone deaf.

Then there was this almighty crashing sound, and the kitchen lit up like Blackpool Illuminations. I was so shit-scared and terrified that I hurled myself for all I was worth at that stupid cat flap, and I burst through the paper and out the other side!

Such was the shock that I bolted for the lounge, disoriented, and was running around, and round barking for all I was worth.

Eventually, Mummee came downstairs, and saw how frightened I was, and carried me back upstairs with her, all the while saying, "it's ok boy, you are safe now, did the thunder and lightning scare you?" Well what do you goddam think, JEEZ. Dad was laughing, and said how did I escape, and when she told him that I must have burst through the stupid newspaper-filled cat flap, he laughed even harder, and said, "well I told you he wouldn't sleep in there for long, but no you said we must do it by the book and we can't have him in our bed, blah blah blah". I was a bit disappointed, if I am honest, at hearing this, as I would've thought it would have been Dad saying no to big bed, but it was Mummee, traitor!

I shall tell you people now, from that day forward I DID NOT SLEEP in the poxy cat-flapped kitchen again, and to teach Mummee a lesson, I farted on her head, ha.

Therefore, I sometimes now get jumpy at loud noises, and hate fireworks. That's right, if you don't know that story (where the fuck, have you been?), I hate them as well, with a vengeance.

Ooo I can hear snake mechanic is going, as Titch is doing her customary "goodbye, good riddance, don't come back anytime soon" bark, HAHA. I shall go and have me some snuggle time with Mummee, maybe Titch will join me and we can snooze together.

Well, all I will say is that Titch and I have now called a second truce, as we both fell asleep on Mummee and it was like dog jenga.

Titch even snored as well, and she said that she hadn't done that for a long time, in fact she couldn't ever remember relaxing that much – she was always on alert.

Mummee has said that she must go out, so we are to be left with Dad. This is somewhat weird, as Dad usually goes to work, but he is off today, which is why smelly mechanic man came. Ooo I wonder where Mummee is going - I'm going to find out.

What, Titch? Well I don't know, I am trying to find out, well come with me then, bark at her, stop her from going, go on, shout, *"MUMMEE, MUMMEE, MUMMEE, WHERE YA GOING, WHERE YA GOING, CAN WE COME, CAN WE COME, CAN WE COME, PLEASE, PLEASE, PLEASE"*.

Oh, it's not worked, as she is going to somewhere you can't take doggies, how bloody selfish is that? So now we are stuck here on a Wednesday with Dad, and the lingering smells of snake mechanic man, and my god Dad has just farted and that smells even worse, good job Mummee isn't here.

Come on Titch, let's terrorise Dad for some fun, are you in? OK, you start, get up on his lap and stare in his face. Well I can't, can I? Slight udderage problem, I need help to get up on the sofa, so you do it. HAHA, she is sitting on his chest staring at his face, he's like, what do you want, Bally? OMG Dad you have said the fatal words, are you an idiot? She will not stop now.

This is fun, we have subjected Dad to an hour of barking and annoying him. Every time he threw the ball for Titch, I then went to up to him with my Monkey Boy toy. He is desperate for Mummee to come back, and said, "Christ you two are like double trouble now, can't we all just have a nice little afternoon nap?"

Oh, ok then, nap time it is, you know how I loves me a little snooze… Come on Titch, enough now, sleepy times. Before I get comfy though, I'll just check the Twitterverse and see what's what.

HA, BF has been drinking I think, her tweets are hilarious. She has actually tweeted a pic of herself fallen over in a bush. I've tweeted back and said WTF, where had she been?

You are not going to believe this, folks, she went to a club with sailor cat, but it was the Pink Flamingo, where her ex, Mr Chicken, now works! BF said there was drama, and it all turned into a big clustercluck! ha ha.

She said she hadn't been in the club long when the main act came on, and she realised with horror that it was "Miss Hen-Rietta", but before she could make an exit, he started to sing to her.

Oooo, I said, what did he sing? Turns out it was her favourite song of all time, "When Doves Cry" UH OH, I remember that song, it was playing when she first met Mr Chicken and she thought he was The One.

She said sailor cat wanted to know who the hell he was, and she said none of your bloody business; he then leapt out of his seat straight towards Miss Hen-Rietta, and scratched his wig off and ripped his dress! It was a horror show, said BF, she had never been so mortified or embarrassed in all her life, not even when she got wedged in a revolving door of the hotel she worked in, and ended up with her bottom in the air.

I am sorry, folks, I started to laugh, so hard that it brought on a wheezing attack - even Titch came in to see if I was ok. I obviously didn't tell BF this, instead I tweeted that maybe it was best she found out now that sailor cat wasn't The One either, and to stay single for a while.

To cheer her up I then tweeted a pic of me singing into a mic, "All the single ladies, all the single ladies, put your hands up, oh you can't", ha ha ha. BF did see the funny side, but said it had saddened her, especially seeing Mr Chicken. She said she was going for a lie down, to nurse her hangover!

Talking of which, Dad is lying prostrate already and Titch is snuggled in next to him. Dad is the only man so far that she really trusts... she still has difficulties with others, but hopefully we can help her overcome this. Awwwwww.... bliss now, I'm snuggled on the other side, ha, Dad is like a double-barrelled dog gun... sssshhhhh now people, snoozing.

Chapter 5   TWAT

Uh oh, Mummee is back, and I don't think she is happy with Dad, as before she left she said to him could he tidy up, but he hasn't done anything. However, in his defence, he did play with us for an hour, then that tired him out, so he snoozed most of the day. I can hear Mummee saying she is a laughing stock at the Doctors now and so doesn't need to come home to him being a twat. Oh God, Mummee is shouting, "you, fat twat" - I hope she doesn't mean me!

Apparently, Mummee thought she had a mole on her chest, I mean, that in itself is super weird having a blind furry creature stuck on your body, but anyhow she went to the doctors to get it checked out, turns out it was a blob of chocolate! Choccomole is now a thing, and my Dad cannot stop laughing.

Dad is antagonizing her now, and still laughing doing a silly dance, I think he's trying to impersonate a choccomole ha ha, this is hilarious, however Mumme thinks he is just being a twat! UH OH they are scaring Titch, STOP IT I must alert them I shall bark,
.

I think Mummee has just realised this and has crouched down to her, which in turn has made her wee herself, NO not Mummee idiots, Titch, haha. Ok, sorry for laughing at you, piss pants, but come on, get a grip.

Dad has gone outside... I may follow, see if I can resurrect my serial killer patch. You coming, Titch? No? Suit yourself.

Ooo this is fun, Dad is in his greenhouse so I am safe to mooch... What do we have here? This looks interesting, I might chew it, yes, I must chew it, oooo god I can't stop myself, I must chew, chew, chew, chew! WHAT, NO, GERROFF, MINE! .... RUPERT, DROP IT, DROP IT... that's my bloody seed hole maker, now give it here... ha ha, Dad can't catch me, I've hidden myself under the bush. This thing just tastes so yummy, and it's good for chewing, helps my teethies, so fuck off.

ARRRGGGGHHHHHHHHHH, ABUSE, HELP! DAD, stop it! He has only gone and grabbed me and pulled me out... Oh CHRIST, here, if it means that much to you have it, I have chewed it enough now anyway. RUPERT look at the state of this now, you've nibbled the end off! YES, and your point is, miserable TWAT? Haha, I can see why Mummee calls you that now, TWAT, TWAT, TWAT...

Hang on, I can hear a strange noise... It's coming from the shed, I must investigate...

FUCK MEEEEEEEE, RUN FOR YOUR LIVES, ARRRRRRRGGGGGGGGGGGGGHHHHHHHH HHHHHH!!!

OMG, there is a giant killer wasp in the shed, and seriously it's like the size of a hand, CALL FOR HELP NOW! I really, really, really hate wasps - they are killers, ninjas in disguise. I got stung once, and ever since I cannot stand them. The story is NOT a funny one.

One summer, I was out mooching and minding my own business, when I needed to do a pooh. I did my customary circling, but just when I went to stoop, I felt THE MOST HORRIFIC PAIN ever, worse than when I had my temperature checked (for those of you who don't know this, again, read my first book, will you?), I was assaulted with no warning and had an object shoved up my rear end, what is it with you hoomans?). Anyway, back to THE PAIN, I actually howled and started running around the garden full pelt, I was like a barking freight train.

Mummee came running to see what the commotion was, and saw me going mental... When she finally caught me and calmed me down, she could see that I had been stung on my privates by a wasp! YES, ON MY DOG PARTS, or what was left of them.

I had them removed, and it was NOT my decision, but I suppose Mummee was being kind, as they can get disease-riddled and we don't want that do we, also it prevents me from bringing any more doggies into the world, as there are enough poor mutts already without homes... In fact, why not go out today and adopt an older doggie? Give it a warm safe home like we did with Titch... Go on, what are you waiting for?

So back to the tale, Mummee gave me a special tablet to help with the pain, and any reactions I may have had, and then bathed my bottom in salt water. It did soothe the pain, and after a while the redness went away, but I got scarred for life and now wasps terrify me, so when I saw that bastard in the shed, well I stress farted and barked loudly. Dad came and said, "Oh come on boy, let's get you inside, and I shall deal with him for you". Aww thank you Dad, I don't think you are a twat really!!

Back inside now, and guess what, yes Titch is in comfy bed, but as I am feeling generous, I shall leave her, and go and see what Mummee is up to...

Mummee, Mummee, what are you doing, when is Nanny going to come? I miss Nanny Hammy and Granddad Potato (he looks like a potato for real, FFS read my book or follow me on Twitter ok?). Oh, hey there Rupe, did you get scared? I heard about that wasp, just like your Mummee aren't you, I don't like 'em either. Oh, by the way, Nanny is coming later for dinner...

Hey people, did you hear that, Nanny is coming later! Whoo hoooo, I might have to do me some serious bum spinning on the rug. [Ssssshh don't say anything, this is super exciting!]

Oi Titch, get up, did you know Nanny is coming later? Well she is, and she brings treats, nom, nom, nom... Erm, excuse me, that is not all I ever think about, food and stuffing my face - I also think about checking Twitter, snoozing, and sleeping. NO it's not the same - snoozing is a light relaxation of the eyelids, but my ears are still alert, whereas sleeping is a full deep body relaxation and everything gets cut off. So, shut up, I have told you, I am like super dog, my IQ is very high.

Just checked Twitter and my PA has tweeted me, asking for a raise. I said she can have a higher chair, ha ha ha. Checked on BF, Stuffy, she has decided to take my advice and stay single for a while, so has ditched sailor cat. Good for her, I said, and besides I will always be there for her.

Tried my luck again with BC, and tweeted her a poem - it said, "Eyes so blue, I love you, give me your heart, and I shall promise not to fart". HA, that ought to do it.

Erm, she tweeted back BAD DOG... hmm, I may have to rethink my wooing techniques.

Well, all this blogging has left me exhausted so it's time for a snooze, and hopefully when I wake up, Nanny and Granddad will be here... Quiet now, sleeping.

Well that was short-lived, story of my life – short, HA! We don't need a doorbell anymore, not with gobshite here. *"WOOF, WOOF, WOOF, WOOF, WOOF, DOOR, DOOR, DOOR, THERE IS SOMEONE AT THE DOOR!"* Alright, calm down, it will be Nanny and Granddad, and that means treat time. Let's do the dance, yes you do know the moves, come on, follow me.

We are killing it people, double whammy wag dance! Titch soon got the hang of it, and Nanny has just melted. I don't mind Titch getting the extra attention today, as I have this big chewy stick, nomm nomm, so I shall report back later...

Hey, you are not going to believe this, all of us, yes ALL of us went to Squirrelly Bastard Park! Granddad had to use a stick (his Arthur's ritus was playing him up), and Nanny was like a slow snail, but still it was brilliant fun. I don't think Titch had ever seen a squirrel bastard before, so I warned her they taunt you a lot.

She went proper mental, barking at everyone and shouting "*bushy-tailed bastards*!" Then she spotted one on the ground, and I swear if that squirrel hadn't spotted her first he would've been squished squirrel! The look in his eyes was hilarious, they like bulged out, never seen anything like it. She was like a ninja though, she crept up to him, and at the last minute he turned and spotted her.

Ha ha, I don't think I have ever laughed so hard, it brought on a wheezing fit. Granddad thought I was having a heart attack, as he had never witnessed it before, but Nanny put him right and said ignore me, I am after attention. PISS OFF NANNY, I am so not...

Mummee and Dad were actually pleasant with each other, and were laughing; it turned out to be the best day ever, but all the excitement has left me exhausted, so yes you've guessed it, snooze time.... come on Titch, let's snuggle, what do you mean NO? Suit yourself... big ZZZZZsssss...

Sssshhhh, it's me Titch. Fatso is snoring his fat little head off, and Nanny and Granddad have gone, so I have sneaked onto his blog. Of course, the idiot didn't put the lock on again, so his IQ can't be very high, can it? Anyway, I have just tweeted this BC and pretended to be Rupert, ha ha, you are gonna love this! I've put a picture of him lying on his back, legs akimbo - he looks like a giant fat grotesque whale - and added the caption, "Come on over to my place and we can play Twister", hee hee hee... Ooo gorra go, I think I can hear him...

Ooo, what a lovely snooze! I don't know where Titch is, but I shall just have me a wander to the kitchen, see if I can get me a treat as I've woken up Hank Marvin (starving), I don't think Nanny and Granddad are here anymore, I guess they couldn't even be bothered to say goodbye to their favourite grandson, turncoat bastards. Bloody Titch really has stolen the limelight.

Mummee is in the kitchen - I am in luck, I shall give her my best doe-eyed look. Mummee, Mummee, it's me, best boy, please give me a treat! Ooooo, she's reaching into the drawer, YES result, nomtastic... She is giving me a chewy stick, and before you lot say anything, you can all piss off - I have decided that the diet is no more.

Yep, you heard right, and I shall tell you why. I have discovered that a rabbit, who hops around all day eating lettuce, only lives until he is 15 years old, whereas a tortoise, who does fuck all, lives until he is 150 years old, so I am now officially a tortoise, judge all you like... I shall still be doing my blog in 100 years' time, whilst you bastards will be six feet under, not judging now are you... WHOA, hang on a minute, I have just had a notification, and it's from BC...

WTF!! I am fuming, you are not going to believe what Titch has gone and done whilst I was snoozing! She tweeted a picture of me with my dangly bits hanging out - and let me tell you, they are not very dangly these days, since the twerps (Mummee and Dad) stole my manhood – and it was a very undignified picture. Well BC has retweeted it, saying, "has everyone seen this? it's a manatee", well charming, I'm sure. She's never going to love me now... Well at least it has had over 40 likes so far, so HA in your face Titch... in fact she is awfully quiet even for her, where is she?

Jesus Christ, what are you doing under there? *I am stuck, don't tell...* Well, I need to, as I can't get you out. Are you an idiot or something, how did you get trapped under the bed? Don't tell me, I can guess - Bally went under there, and you thought you could fit and fetch it.

I shall go and alert Mummee, but I am surprised she hasn't looked for you already, how long have you been under there? Alright, alright, calm down, how did I know you can't tell the time? I mean you speak fucking German, but can't tell the time - you are truly an idiot of epic proportions... What was that? I can't hear you... *"Wait until I get out!"* Ooo

I'm scared, look at me shaking in my fur (I AM scared, but don't tell her).

MUMMEEEEEEEEEE, MUMMEEEE, where are you? Oh, for god's sake, no wonder she didn't know Titch was missing, lazy cow is snoozing on the sofa. I need to alert her, I shall bark, here goes: "WOOOF, WOOOF, WOOOF!" What's that Rupert, there's been an accident? has Titch fallen down the mine? Ha, why was it always a mine shaft in the programme Skippy the Kangaroo? WAKE UP MUMMEE, Titch needs our help, and no she has not fallen down a mine.

Hey Rupe, what are you after, not another chewy stick? The answer is NO... Why are you barking at me, what, why are you going upstairs? Jesus Christ Mummee, you can be so stupid sometimes, will you just follow me up the stairs? Titch is stuck under the goddam bed. Oh, you get the message now, do you? Well thank Christ for that.

Come on then, let's see what's up here, hey I wonder where your sister is...? TITTCCH, OH MY GOD, how on earth did you get trapped under there, bloody hell... Right, hang on, let me lift the bed a little, OOMPF, ready...
Come on now girlie, out you get.

YES, FREEDOM! I thought my days were numbered, thanks for saving me Rupert... One thing's for sure, Mummee doesn't clean very often up here, sooooo many dust bunnies... Ha, OMG, don't you say anything, don't you dare.

Come here, Titch, are you alright, my little princess? I didn't even know you had gone missing... Good boy Rupert here, he must have known, as he came and alerted me, how clever are you, my little boy? *OH he's clever alright, fat bastard, couldn't even fit under to get me out, and so I had to tell him to fetch you, but you praise him, the fat fucking tortoise.* Hey, if it wasn't for me fetching Mummee, you would still be stuck, so shut your gob. Right, shall we go for a walk, as it looks a lovely afternoon?

Hang on, where was Dad when all this drama unfolded? Oh right, he is still in his precious greenhouse, planting up for the summer - I hope strawberries, they are my fave. I shall have to have a wander out there when we get back from the walk.

Back later folks, off to terrorize the neighbourhood.

Chapter 6 : My Twitter Family

Folks, hang on to your bladders, because you are not going to believe what Titch did on the walk earlier! Even Mummee was mortified and had to rein her in, ha ha.

We spotted Ginger Bastard, and Titch's past experiences of him have been somewhat traumatic... The first encounter, anyone would think she had been punched by Mike Tyson, such was the wailing sound she made. So, when we saw him (Ginger Bastard, not Mike) today I was ready to protect her, that's what you do isn't it?

There he was licking away at his nuts, dirty bastard, leg raised above his head, like some kind of zen yoga freak... Seriously, how do cats do that? I am lucky now if I can raise my leg to pee, and half the time I don't bother nowadays, what with my Arthur's ritus (yeah, I have that, same as Granddad). Anyway, Ginger Bastard looked up, ready to strike, with such contempt on his face. But as for what came next, well I was astounded.

Titch firstly started shouting in German at him, "*HOSENSCHEISSER!*" really loudly (it means coward or trouser-shitter). Ha ha, how apt, I thought, as Ginger Bastard shits in the house in a tray! Then she walks right up to him and swipes at him with her paw, knocking him sideways. I have never laughed so hard, but Mummee was horrified.

She started yanking Titch in on her lead, shouting NO, and Ginger Bastard was so shocked he just lay there looking dazed. It was hilarious! I thought, yes, let that be a lesson to you, you cannot go around bullying people. I was so proud of my sister at that moment, and to show her how much I went over to her and licked her nose.

She liked that, and said she found some newfound strength and was not going to live her life in fear anymore, so the first brave thing she wanted to do was tackle Ginger Bastard for swiping at her with his claw. Well, I said, you sure did show him, ha ha!

On our way back, we noticed a newbie cat, however, at first, I had to do a double take and make sure my bionic eyes were not deceiving me, as he/she looked like an ornament at first. This cat was sitting so still in the window that I couldn't be sure it was real, so I waddled up to the window and barked a little. Still nothing, it just sat still as a statue.

It was very sleek looking, and black and white. I don't know its name as I couldn't talk through the glass, but eventually he (for some reason I think it's a male) turned his head very slowly and narrowed his eyes at me, as if to say, and who the fuck, are you, and get off my property. We shall have to keep an eye out for him. In the meantime, I shall nickname him Dummy, ha ha, like the ones you see in shop windows.

We are back home and Titch is going crazy, something about paper and yellow... WHAT? WILL YOU TAKE THE BALL OUT OF YOUR MOUTH? Right, now tell me again, calmly. *A boy with a yellow bag has delivered a newspaper!* Yes and, oh really, you don't like yellow, why? *The nasty man used to wear a fluorescent jacket and it sparked something off in me. I am sorry, I shall try in future not to bark at the paperboy!*

Come on, let's go outside and see what Mum is doing. I think she might be helping Dad plant up the strawberries for this year, and boy when they start to come through the smell is incredible, you will be sure to love them.

You mean to tell me you have never had a strawberry? OMG, poor you! Well they are delicious and yummy, and we can eat them... No, they are not ready yet, they have to grow, they will be ready in about three months... Of course ,you will still be here then, don't be stupid. OUCHIE! Well you are not going anywhere now, are you? I am stuck with you.

I shall see if I can get Mummee to get us some so you can taste them, ok, how's that? Right, I am off to check Twitter and see what's been happening, do you want to tweet something? *CAN I?* Yes, come on.

Titch has tweeted a pic of herself with a tiara on, and called herself Princess Titch. I must admit she has got a very beautiful face, oh that reminds me, I need to tweet BC and see if I can get her attention today...

Well that should do it, I am certain of it. I posted a video clip of me looking rather dashing, having my beard brushed with Basil (my brushy thing that Mummee uses). I likes having me a good brush – it's very relaxing, and I look handsome after.

I am sure she is going to love that - I shall wait to see if I get a reply. I also tweeted my BF Stuffy. She said Mr Chicken has left his job at the Pink Flamingo, and has decided to quit being a drag queen for now, as his heart was all of a flutter when he saw Stuffy again. I said be very wary, you got burned once (not literally, jeez, Stuffy would ignite like a cheap sofa) - no, but her feelings were badly hurt, and it took me ages to console her. She did say that she was meeting him for a drink at some hotel, and would keep me posted. I have a feeling this is going to go bad.

PING, ooo I have a reply from BC... WTF no way, she actually liked my video, and said I looked alright for a fat idiot! I am in love, I don't think I have ever been called a fat idiot by such a stunning broad, wowzers! I need to reconsider the diet malarkey perhaps, if I am to win her affections.

Hang on, what now? For Christ sake, you and that ball of yours, well where is it now? How the hell did it get under there? Well I am not getting it. I don't like the shed at the moment, there was a killer wasp in it last time I looked, so you will have to alert Mummee. Hopefully she can reach it for you, otherwise you shall have to go into therapy, ha ha.

Mummee, Mummee, Titch has lost her ball under the shed, help her please! "Hey Titch, what is wrong, why are you crying at the shed? and where is Rupert, come on, time to go in now. No, you don't want to? In fact, where is your ball? OH, have you lost it under the shed? Don't worry, Mummee will get it." Thank CHRIST FOR THAT! *Is our Mummee an idiot, Rupert? I mean how difficult is it to communicate that my ball is stuck under the shed - why else would I be staring at it like some kind of shed freak?*

UH OH, don't let on you called Mummee an idiot! *ERM, I didn't, technically I said IS she, not SHE is. Pay attention Fatso, I thought your IQ was high, so far you have proved yourself to be schwachsinnig!* OOO what's that, genius? *NO, it means IDIOTIC, ha ha ha ha ha.*

You are such a meanie, I am going now to claim comfy bed for my afternoon snooze, and I do not want to be disturbed by your neediness, ok?

Actually. before I have a nap, I may as well check the Twitterverse and see if there is any more news from Stuffy or BC, and also post a few tweets of wisdom, as I am renowned for being a philosopher. Oooo my PA has sent me a message and wants to know if she can have a day off. I tweeted back and said ok, but don't let it happen again, HA, and I tweeted this quote: "Legends don't die.... I am a living example!"

Twitter is so funny, it's like a little family, and I have lots of new followers. I am sure it's because of my handsome good looks, nothing to do with Titch joining my account, of course. In fact, one of my many adoring fans recently sent me a toy! Vicki is her name, the fan not the toy... Jeez, I am not some kind of sex pervert, it was not that sort of toy!

It was in fact a pheasant, which was supposed to squeak, but it didn't ... Thanks Vicki, great present, just send me your cast offs, HA! To be fair, it was a great gift, and Mr P and I got along just fine - I ripped that bastard's stuffing out in less than thirty minutes flat! I tweeted a pic of me with him, looking all smug.

The other new follower is a broad called Viv, she complains about everything, but she is funny, and, also likes to observe other humans, she is a huge fan of that funny man Mummee loves, oh what's his bloody name? I know the cat's name (BC), but can't for the life of me remember his... Anyway, he is such a kind generous human, he does lots for animals, and so I now follow him too.

I tweeted a pic of me with hearts all around my head and said would she be mine, my sweet valentine? Together we can make music.

All I got back was a resounding NO. She is proving to be a very tough nut to crack; I shall have to rethink my wooing. Well that is enough tweeting for one day - you can become a little obsessed with it all, and even though I love our little "Twitter Family" and all my adoring fans, you do have to take time out, so I'm off for that snooze now!

FFS, Titch is in my bed, snoring her head off... Right, time to get my own back, methinks. I have videoed her, and good god, she sounds like a snoring walrus - I shall keep that for later. As for now, I suppose I shall just lie here on the floor and wait for Mummee to lift me up on the sofa.

I didn't have to wait too long, and now I am snuggled next to Mummee for some snooze time. Titch is still in comfy bed, and Dad is.... well, who cares? zzzzzzzzzzz

Well Dad has gone out, I think I heard Mummee mention something about fetching some topsoil for the garden - no idea what that is, and to be honest I don't care. I am in need of a walk, food and checking Twitter, in that order. Oi Titch, come on, it's walkies time! *Ooooo really? I love our outings now, we get to meet so many idiots, and I can use more of my German, ready? Eins, zwei, drei...* What is that? *One, two, three, dumbo!*

Well I am not to know, and stop calling me dumbo - I am sure he was an elephant with big ears. *Exactly, HA! Oh, come on, I am only joking Rupert, you know I love you now! Let's get going, we have some teasing to do together, and if I spot Ginger Bastard, he had better look out.*

That was some walk! I was so proud of Titch, who now has a little spring in her step. We spotted Ginger Bastard, but he took one look at Titch and fled over his fence - it was like watching a flying ginger ball of fur. We walked past the house with the weird Dummy cat, who was still sitting, still as a waxwork, in his window. Only his eyes gave him away, slanted and sly.

Titch was now pumped, she jumped up the window at him, and OMG I didn't think cats could fly, but that bastard jumped five feet off his windowsill and scarpered out of sight! It was hilarious - Titch was laughing so hard, she made this hacking sound, so of course Mummee panicked and thought she was choking.

Titch soon realised this was how to gain extra attention from Mummee, and whispered to me, *does she always fuss over you when you are laughing*? I said yes, because Mummee doesn't know we are laughing. *Noted*, she said.

She also got to use more German when we spotted Henry. You remember him, foul breath, lab experiment cross between a bull and a dog, poor sod… Well, we rounded the corner and there he was, cocking his leg in a rather wobbly fashion. Titch spied him and shouted loudly, "*Furz Atem!*" Of course Henry didn't know what she was on about, and good job, because it means fart breath, OMG.

So, all in all a rather entertaining walk. I must say I do like walkies even more now with Titch, it really livens them up! Back home now and food time, nomm nomm, can't talk, dog eating. Titch, I have told you a million times already, you don't have to gobble it down so fast, it will make you sick! Calm down, it's ok, I promise I won't eat it!

Just off to check Twitter, why don't you come and tweet a pic? Come on, tell them some

German, they will be amazed that you are so clever!

OOO, look Titch we have another new follower, a lovely kind lady called Jeannie and her cat Casper. He looks like me, all white fur. *HA HA, I don't think so Fatso, for starters look how sleek he is compared to you.*

Erm, do you want to tweet or not? Tweet them a joke in German, but make it funny, I don't want you ruining my reputation. *Ha, what reputation is that, fat idiot?*

I don't want to do a German joke, they are all about sausages and they are the Wurst! Ha ha.

OMG you are quite funny, now gerroff, go on, you are stealing the limelight. Time for me to tweet BC and see if I can get her attention today.

Right, I have done a little poem, and included a picture of me looking cute. My eyes are huge, like currant bun eyes. If she doesn't fall for me now, I have no chance. It went like this:

My heart beats faster every time I see your face
With those cute little ears and dazzling eyes
I am definitely going to spruce myself up and give up the pies!

Let's see what response I get to that... In the meantime, I have tweeted Stuffy, and asked if she has heard any more from Mr Chicken.

BC tweeted back, rather quickly, oooo this could be a sign! You are not going to believe this, she has responded with her own little ditty, and said this:

Fat Sausage Fat Sausage see how you run, With your udders bouncing and a face like a bun!

Well I cannot believe it. Firstly, I am not a sausage, and secondly how on earth did she know my udders bounce when I run? I am mortified! Oh, piss off Titch, it's far from funny. *I know, it's actually freaking hilarious, sausage boy, ha ha! I like this cat, she has style! I may tweet her myself, see if we can be friends, then I can tell her all about your bad habits.* Oi gerroff, now and go and find your goddam bally, you weirdo.

Ppppffft, this incident has actually caused me to stress fart. I am very upset... Ooooo, what's this? A message from BF, let's see what she has to say.

UH OH, this isn't good, she is surrounded by chocolate wrappers and empty wine bottles, and her tweet says, Stuff it all! Oh oh, I shall have to find out what has happened.

Well after having a long private conversation with Stuffy, I have learned that she went out with Mr Chicken for a drink and a meal, however because of his stint at the Pink Flamingo they kept getting interrupted by adoring fans, and it was all too much for Stuffy, so she got drunk, fell off the chair and rocked herself to sleep! Mr Chicken had to carry her back to her apartment, and some of her stuffing came out, and she was so mortified that she spent the weekend in a drunken chocolate haze.

I told her not to be so hard on herself and that I am sure Mr Chicken had seen her in a worse state when they lived together, but she said no, never - she always kept it dignified. Oh dear, poor Stuffy! It was bad last time when they broke up, but this is something new. I said, well I am here for you if you need me.

All this drama has left me hungry, I think I need to wander to the kitchen and see if Mummee is in there with any offerings... Hey Titch, have you seen Mummee, is she in the kitchen? *Oh hang on, let me just use my telepathic skills and find out for you...* Wow, can you do that really? *Don't be a fat idiot, of course I can't, dumbo! Go and see for yourself, I am not your slave.* Meanie, bloody hell, it's a trek to the kitchen, ooommpff, ok I'll just plonk myself here in the doorway, and see what's what.

Rupert, why on earth have you plonked yourself there, I could've tripped over you, you're like a big bloody furry rug. Come on, get out of the way! NO, not until you give me a treat, Hey, that is molestation, gerroff my udders, HELP, ABUSE! You can stop laughing Titch, where did you suddenly spring from? You are like a bloody stealth ninja.

Well that was a disaster. Not only did I not get a treat, but Mummee shoved me out the way like I was a sack of potatoes, and where's Dad when you need him, still out. Well screw you all, I am going for a snooze.

Oh my god, he is such a baby, he is sulking now in his comfy bed... well I shall take this opportunity to write in his blog, and tell you all a tale of when I was stuck in the kennel with my German pal. The nights used to be the worst, all the other dogs howling and crying. I hated every minute of it, but like I say, good job I had Fitz, he kept me safe and taught me German.

So anyway, this one night, all the staff had gone for the night, except the night watchman. It was incredibly dark, and I remember it was raining, because you could hear the rain splattering on the roof. It was really lashing down - it drove the other doggies crazy.

Fitz started to pace, and I said, what's wrong pal, you seem agitated, and he said he could sense something was wrong, and could smell it in the air. I am not going to lie, I was petrified - my hackles were standing up on end, and I was quivering in the corner. I thought maybe the evil bastard who dumped me had come back.

Fitz suddenly stopped pacing and just stood as still as a statue by the bars of our enclosure, sniffing the air. He then whispered to me in German, so as not to panic the others, "FEUER", which means fire!

I said to him, are you sure Fitz, and he said yes, he would know the smell anywhere, as he was an old firearms dog and recognised the burning smell of explosives. He said we *needed to remain calm, but try and get the others to bark, to alert the night watchman.*

I said leave it to me! I was so brave, I jumped onto Fitz's back and started to shout jokes, which I knew would cause laughter amongst the others, and laughter sounds like barking to humans, which in turn I hoped would alert the night watchman. I prayed it would work, as I didn't fancy being crispy dog.

It worked! All the dogs started laughing. Some were even shouting, "oi shut up Titch, we are trying to sleep", but this increased the sounds of their barks, and before long the lights went on and the night watchman came in. He saw the fire, which fortunately hadn't taken hold yet and was still contained in the bin. Some idiot had smoked a cigarette, and it hadn't been put out right (this was before smoking was banned). The night watchman quickly put out the fire, and then sat with us for the rest of the night, to make sure everyone calmed down and slept well. He paid special attention to me and Fitz, and gave us both a treat. He said what an amazing dog Fitz was, and that he should get an award for alerting him.

I agreed, Fitz was incredible. To this day I will never ever forget Fitz, and how he saved us all from possible death! It wasn't long after that episode that a family heard about his bravery and came along to visit him; they fell in love straight away, and he was rehomed with them. The look he gave me though as he left will stay in my heart forever, as we exchanged a silent message in German: Ich werde Sie nie vergessen. Bleiben Sie stark. (I will never forget you. Stay strong.)

And that is all for now, as remembering him always brings a little sadness to my heart. Even though I know he is in his forever home like me, I just miss his strong voice....

OMG WHAT - gerroff, my blog now, I didn't say you could type in it! What babble have you been writing now? Some more shit stories about me, I bet...

OH, I have just read what Titch wrote, and even I have a lump in my throat. This Fitz sounds like such a brave doggie, how great would it be if I could find him on Twitter and reconnect them! In fact,I am going to make that my mission.

Right, I have tweeted a request to everyone, can they help find Fitz, if he is out there. Sssshhh, don't tell Titch, I want it to be a surprise if we find him. Oh, good grief, what is she barking at now? SHURRRUP, it's only Dad, back from wherever he has been.

Come on, let's go terrorize him in the garden, ha. *Rupert, what is Dad doing, he is carrying lots of bags of something and he looks a little red in the face! Is he ok?* Yeah, don't worry, he gets like that - out of condition, Mummee says... She also said he needs to lose some weight – "fat twonk" I think she called him once, they didn't speak then for the whole day! Don't worry, you will get used to seeing his face that colour. I know it's alarming at first - when I first saw him like that, I shouted for somebody to call an ambulance, as I thought he was dying, HAHA! Right, I think I hear Mummee calling us, must be time for a walk, come on.

OOOOO, it looks like the usual suspects are out today... There's Douglas, the yapping idiot, thankfully he hasn't seen us... oh and look who it is, haven't seen him for a while, Ian Beagle! I wonder if he has one paw smaller than the other, oh that was Jeremy Beagle wasn't it? I'm getting mixed up, HA!

Hey Rupert, who the hell is that? I don't like the look of her, right snooty-looking bitch... Oh that's Pomerbitch, I can never remember her real name, but she is quite snooty, thinks she is something special. Shout some German at her for a laugh. *Oh ok...Ihre Mutter säugt Schweine... ha ha ha ha!*

OMG what did you shout? She's gone mental - that high- pitched barking means she is really annoyed. *I said your Mom suckles pigs, ha!*

Ha ha, well, she didn't like that... Oh hang on, she is shouting something at you... What's that? I can't understand you, come closer...

"LECK MICH AM ARSCH!"

Oops, looks like she knows German, Titch, what did she say? SHE SAID WHAT? That is disgusting, nobody wants to lick your arse! Gerroff, get out of here, dirty bitch.

Well I never, I knew that Pomerbitch was a fake, pretending like she was some snooty lady, when all along she was a foul-mouthed little tramp. Come on Titch, it's time to go home now, that's enough trouble-making for one day.

I agree, and I cannot believe the filthy mouth on that bitch! I hope I don't run into her again. I hope we get a treat when we get back - I am starving, my appetite has returned, which means I am less stressed now... That can only be a good thing, so you, Fatso, can watch out.

Whatever do you mean?

Oh, looks like we have bombed out Titch, Mummee isn't going to give us anything...

Come on, let's check Twitter instead, it's more fun anyway.

Chapter 7 – I'm a poet and I didn't know it

Well, that was fun, spent the last hour on Twitter, just tweeting back and forth with all our furry friends. My paws are aching though now... At one point, I had to shove Titch out of the way, as I have had a message from someone who thinks they might know Fitz. This is super exciting.

Also, I spotted a tweet from a book club - they are running a competition for the best poem. I might have to enter, as my wit and humour know no bounds.

Whatcha doing Rupe? I want to tweet something, I'm bored and Mummee is helping Dad with something. Well you can't, I'm busy doing important stuff now, so bugger off, go and play with Bally in the garden. I won't be long, ok?

You are so up your own arse sometimes, thinking you are like super important, well, you Dummkopf, I am going to find Mummee.

Right, Mad Bitch has gone, I can now read what this message says… ooo interesting, they say that Fitz doesn't have a Twitter account, but is on something called Facebook – his new owners set up a page to honour his bravery, and he has lots of followers. OMG this is brilliant, they have included a link to his page and they say I can message him.

I am soooooooo excited! I cannot wait for Titch to know I have found Fitz, but first I better message him.

What will I say? Ok, got it, this is what I said:

Hello Fitz, my name is Rupert. You don't know me, but I believe you spent some time in a kennel with my new sister Titch. She's a little Jack Russell who's a bit crazy!

She talks about you all the time, and I know she would love it if she could be back in contact with you.

If you remember her and want to discuss, then please message me back.

All I can do now is wait... ppppffft, oops sorry, it's the nervous excitement of waiting to hear.

Ok, let's go and see where she is whilst I am waiting. Oi Titch, Tiiiittcchhh, TIIITTTCCHHH! Where the hell is she now? OMG, are you mentally challenged, or just a super idiot? *Listen up Fatso, I cannot get out to smack you right now, but I am neither, This, was not my fault. Now, are you going to help or not?*

Well, I just don't know how you have managed to get stuck under the SOFA, of all places! I mean WTF, explain this to me please. Oh, and by the way, it's weird just talking to your nose, ha! It's poking out and looks like a button.

Enough questions, and aww thanks, I do have a cute nose, don't I? Right, go and tell Mummee that I am trapped under the reclining sofa, which, may I add, was fully reclined when I came in, with Dad lying on it. My bally got stuck under it and I thought it was safe to crawl in and get it. I was WRONG.

Dad didn't know I had crawled under it, so, when Mummee shouted at him to come and help her with something, he pressed the button to recline it down. I tried barking, but the sound must have been muffled by Bally (which was in my mouth). And the next thing I know, I am stuck under this sofa. So now you're here - go and alert them, ok?

Jeez, you do get yourself into some situations, bloody hell! Right, I am off to find them, be back soon - don't go anywhere, will you? HA HA HA. *Very funny, Fatso.*

Where are Mummee and Dad? I shall bark, that usually gets their attention if I do it loud enough... WOOF, WOOF, WOOF, nope, not working, time for howling methinks... HA, that's done it! Mummee is running downstairs, shouting, "what's wrong with Rupert?", Dad is behind her. Erm they look a bit red, oh NOOOOOO I hope they haven't been doing that thing that hurts my eyes, yuck!

Hey Rupert, what's wrong, little fella, and where is your sister? Erm, stuck under the sofa, and if you two hadn't been doing what I think you were doing, then you would've known this. The words NEGLECT AND ABUSE spring to mind, I shall have to call that animal abuse hotline... Right, now I'm barking at the sofa, "oi Titch, can you drop

Bally, and make some noise, so Mummee and Dad know you are stuck".

Ok, woof, woof, woof, WOOF, WOOF, WOOF, for Christ sake, I am stuck under here, idiots.

Thank god, it's working. Mummee is shouting at Dad, "how on earth did you not know that she was trapped under there, you are an absolute dick, FFS, she could have been crushed! I cannot believe this. Come on Titch, my baby girl, it's ok sweetheart. Is Dad a stupid TWAT? Yes, he is."

Blimey, how on earth did I know she had crawled under there, and why didn't she bark when I started lowering the chair, idiot dog. *OI DAD, I am here you know, and I am far from an idiot, gggggrrrr.* Look, now you've upset her, come on, let's see what treats we have, poor thing.

Ha in your face Fatso, I get a treat, fuss and affection, you get ZILCH. Best day ever.

You will be apologising to me very soon, and regret calling me Fatso, when you know what I have done. *OOO tell me, tell me, tell me!* NOPE not yet, bugger off now, you baby girl HA.

Oi, only Mummee can call me that! Anyway, here, have some of my treat, ok? Thanks for coming to my rescue again, you are a good brother really.

Awww, thank you... Right, I have to go and check Twitter, so I need you to stay out of trouble, ok? *OK!*

I am so excited to see if there is a message yet from Fitz. How awesome will it be if he remembers, and wants to talk to Titch? She will be so happy.

You are not going to believe it, this is super exciting news! I have a message, just have to make sure that Titch isn't anywhere in the vicinity... Right, the coast is all clear, let's see what it says...

Hi there Rupert, this is Fitz, I must admit it was quite a shock to read your message to me, but it was also very exciting, as yes of course I remember Titch, how could I forget? We shared a "cell" for many months, and she kept me sane, what with her jokes and story-telling.

I would love to speak with her, do you know if you or your Mummee has Skype? It lets you video link each other live and talk... It would be so good to see her again. Anyway Rupert, let me know if you can link up, I await your reply.

Best wishes

Fitz

OMG, OMG, OMG, I must find out if Mummee has this Skype he is on about, but how? And I can now tell Titch! I cannot wait to see her face, this is the best news ever.

Tiiiiiittttcccccchhhhhh, where are you? And please don't tell me you are stuck somewhere again... *whadda you want Fatso, I am here in the lounge under comfy bed, can't you see me, or are you blind?* I am NOT blind - I have told you like a million times, I have bionic eyes - and why on earth are you under comfy bed? Oh, don't bother, forget I asked... Listen, I have some very, very exciting news for you, so come out from under there and I shall tell you.

OOOO, you have me all intrigued now, what is it, a new collar? Ooo no, no, I know, my own comfy bed.... Nooooo? Wait, I've got it, a coat

*for when it's cold? I'm right, it's a coat. I can
see from your face.*

It's none of those, so will you just SHUT UP?
Ouch, you will regret that. Right, listen, do
you remember Fitz? *WHAT a stupid question,
of course I do, idiot.* Well a few days ago, after
you told the story of the fire, it got me
thinking, and I thought I wonder if Fitz is on
Twitter, and if so, how great would it be if you
could talk to him again.

*OMG, is he on Twitter? That is awesome, give
me his Twitter account now, I must talk to
him!* No, he's not on Twitter... *Why would you
tease me like that, Fatso?* Well if you hang on
and let me finish - I tweeted a message to
everyone asking if they could help find him,
and somebody came back to say that he had
a Facebook account, as he was a local hero,
and his Mum and Dad do a lot for animals
who don't have homes.

I knew he would end up famous, and with a loving family, this is brilliant news! What else did you find out, are we on this Facebook thingy? Well, firstly no, we don't have an account, but I did track him down and sent him a message, and guess what? *WHAT?* He replied to me just now and says he wants to talk with you, and if we have something called Skype, we can even do a live video with each other! How fucking brilliant is that, and in fact how fucking brilliant am I, EH, EH???

Why are you crying? OMG, stop it, Mummee will come in and think I've made you cry! *I'm sorry, I am so overwhelmed, Rupert, this has to be the best, most wonderful thing anyone has ever done for me. Your kindness is incredible, and I love you bruvver, my little Fatso. Thank you, from the bottom of my heart.*

Alright, alright, enough with the dramatics, we need to figure out if we have this Skype thingy, and then we can message him back and set it up, ok? *OK.* Right, let me just message my BF Stuffy, she might know where this Skype thingy is on the computer, and then I don't have to pester Mummee.

Ok, so I have messaged Stuffy. I hope she has got over the other night when she embarrassed herself with Mr Chicken, he seriously isn't worth her time, but I can't tell her and lord knows I've tried.

Oh, also tweeted BC, whilst I was on Twitter, and said I knew her birthday was coming up soon, in July, and would she like me to wine and dine her? She tweeted back, "sorry Fatso, I'm busy on that day". Rude!

I must enter that poetry contest, I have composed a little ditty, this is what I have so far:

Mom thinks I resemble a bear,
I checked images and I don't think this is fair
-
Bears are black, brown or white;
Mom needs to check out her eyesight,
Maybe she is colour blind, or the likeness is all in her mind;
I am after all a Jack Russell of sorts who wrote a book;
It's on Amazon now, so why not take a look?
My first book was a diary of trying to lose weight,
But at nearly 12 years old I think I have left it too late;
I'm still fat and round and I don't know why -
I have two small meals a day (plus two treats, I won't lie);
To reduce my weight I've tried and tried,
But I'm still fat and round and now mystified.

Well, I might send it in, but then again, it could do with some tweaking, so will come back to it later. For now, I am patiently waiting to hear from Stuffy, about this Skype thingy.

Oh, while I am waiting, did I ever tell you about my Mummee and her bad clouds? No? Well I shall, but don't say anything ok, she gets embarrassed. Sometimes Mummee has these clouds that hang over her, she calls them her sad clouds, and these clouds follow her everywhere, sometimes for a few days.

When she sees them coming, and recognises them she will often say to me, Oh, my Boy I love you so much, come here and let me give you a cuddle, and of course I oblige I love being cuddled by Mummee. She doesn't have these clouds days often, but when she does, it's like everything becomes, a task, and she becomes super sensitive to everything, I think I heard her once, say to Nanny it was called anx high tea or something, I don't really know some words, but I do know that I calm her, and this makes me feel really good and proud that I help, as it's not a very nice thing to have.

I think lots of humans suffer with it, I overheard her talking with Dad, he doesn't have it, but is very understanding, and talks to Mummee and makes her see things sensibly, instead of them over whelming her, which sometimes things can.

She takes, lots of walks and reads a lot which also helps, as it her focuses her mind elsewhere and not trapped inside her own head as she says, well don't tell her I've shared this, as she feels silly ok.. ooo I have a notification and it's from Stuffy.

This is excellent news, BF has told me where the skype button thing is and so I don't have to bother Mummee and I can set it up so we can talk to Fitz. Hey Titch, come here, *WHAT, I am busy,* forget it, I was only going to tell you that we can skype Fitz.

I'M COMING I'M COMING …I am here, whoo hoo this is the best day ever, right what do we have to do fatso, come on, come on, I can't wait to see Fitz's face.

Just have a little patience, ok, so I have to fiddle with this, set that up, press this, and call, ooooo its ringing hey what a weird sound it makes, like it's under water, or when I fart in the bath ha ha ha , blimey it's taking a long time, what if he's not in, I have no idea how this is supposed to work.

Hello, Hello, HEELLLLLOOOOOOO, can you see me, *OMG Jesus H Christ, It's Fitz, it's really him, Hey Fitz I'm here can you see me, wave your paw, ha look Rupert he's waving his paw,* Right, shall I leave you too to catch up and when your done shout me ok I'm off to check Twitter, on my phone as you are on here and then a snooze me thinks.

Hey Fitz, is that really you buddy, I cannot believe my eyes, I'm welling up here, it only seems like yesterday that we were in that god forsaken place, how are you, what has been happening, you look amazing.

Take a breath Titch, you don't change do you, hundred miles an hour, calm yourself little one, remember what I used to say to you ruhiger Geist zu beruhigen, *Yes Calm Mind Calm Spirit, I still use it now as my mantra, however it didn't work not so long back I had a terrible flashback.* Oh why what happened, not about that bastard who dumped you, *yes him, but I don't want to discuss that now, I want to hear all about you, and what you've been doing, and oh my, I am so happy to have found you again Fitz.*

Right, it's me Rupert, in case you are confused, I have left them to it, so I have checked Twitter, and BC has lost her catberry, so being the good kind doggie that I am, I have sent her an upgrade of an icat, I hope she likes it.

Thanked BF for helping me with the skype fingy, and she asked what it was for, when I told her she started to cry, I said I didn't think she could cry, but she said yes, only it comes out as stuffing, so doesn't do it very often. OMG! I said well stop crying now, it's all happy news.

She said that her and Mr Chicken, had come to a decision to remain just friends, and she was fine with this, and actually went out for a pizza with him, of course she didn't eat any of hers, just sat staring at it!!

PING!, yes that's right a new notification has come through, let me just check it, OH MY GOOD GOD, everyone stop the press, you are not going to believe this, in fact I cannot believe it myself,

BC is following ME BACK, yep you heard that right, she tweeted saying that I as I had sent her an icat and it was the kindest thing anyone had done, she has decided to follow me, and said she hoped she wouldn't regret it.

Well I can tell you all now, I will make sure she doesn't regret it, this, has to be the MOST EXCITING thing that has ever happened to me, I am thrilled, right time for a tweet to her I think.

I just tweeted, a pic of my face looking super happy, and I said you have just made a little dog even happier. Wow, she's responded saying GOOD DOG. Heaven, I'm in heaven tra la la la la la la

Ok, let's go and check on Titch, as it's been over an hour and so I wonder if they are still talking. Titch, Titch, TIIITTTCCCCCHHHHHH, where the hell is she now, Jesus Christ, this broad is a nightmare, I left her rabbiting away on that skype thing, now that's switched off and there is no sign of her.

BOO, ha ha ha, you have just jumped nearly as high as that dummy cat, should see your face, Why would you do that, I've stress farted now, so that serves you right, where were you anyway, *I was hiding behind the curtain, as I heard you waddling in, and I just*

knew you would think I had got myself stuck somewhere, ha ha.

Well, it wasn't funny, anyhow, what happened with your skype thing, with Fitz, and are you staying in touch now. *Oh Rupert, I am so grateful to you, it was the best conversation ever, and seeing him again, brought a lump to my throat, but the great news is, he is so happy now and lives a sedate comfy live, his Mum and Dad do a lot for abandoned animals, and it's all done through his Facebook page, he's the avocado,* HA HA HA, don't you mean advocate.

What did I call him then, I think it's a food, green and mushy inside, looks disgusting, don't worry I get words jumbled sometimes, I won't hold it against you!

Anyway, as I was saying, he was so happy to hear from me, and glad that I am now in a safe forever home, he said that he couldn't believe it when he read your message and got quite emotional, which for him, is a big deal, as when we were in that place together, he never once showed me his softer side, always on alert, always strong, and brave, all to protect me.

We had a good long chat, and he said for me to call him anytime, he has also said it might be easier to message him sometimes on his Facebook, as he can't always get on the skype, so messages are easier. It was brilliant to be back in touch with him, thank you so much Rupe, you really are the best, and I love you, now come on let's stop with all the sentimental emotional crap and go out on a walk and do some terrorising.

Aww Titch, I love you too, and yes come on I can hear our leads jangling, let's go and have some fun., Hey, before we go did you know that next month is my birthday, we can celebrate, and get everyone in our Twitter family to join in the fun, what do you say ?

Yeah, that sounds like a great plan, I don't even know when my birthday is, in fact I have never had a birthday celebration before, but what the hell, let's celebrate yours in style. Hang on, you don't know when you were born?, *no, I told you my story, I don't even know who my parents are, anyway it's no big deal its ok.*

NO, NO, NO, it is a big deal, so I shall forgo my birthday, and how about we say that your birthday is 2nd July, that's only a couple of weeks away, and we can announce it on Twitter, and have a party, what do think.

OMG, really, that would be frigging awesome, I could dress up and everything, YES, this is the best day ever. Thank-you, Rupert, from the bottom of my heart, you are so kind.

Chapter 8;   The Gift Of Giving

Well I have changed my mind about the stupid poetry competition - I have bigger things to focus on, and that's organising Titch's birthday for her, as she has never had one.

If I send out a tweet to all the Twitter family explaining that it is Titch's first real birthday, maybe they can come up with ideas for how to celebrate. In the meantime, I have decided to run an auction for a pawsonally (!) signed copy of my first book, Diary of a Fat Jack Russell, and the money I raise can go to the winner's charity of choice. How brilliant am I? The gift of giving creates such a wonderful feeling.

Right, the auction is all set - I have tweeted a pic of me with the book signed by my very own paw, which took me ages may I add! I have asked everyone to retweet, and have said that the auction will run for twenty-four hours. I am super excited! I wonder how much it will make, lots I hope, as it's for a very good cause, saving animals.

Now that's all done, I just need to message everyone about Titch's birthday. But first I need to stretch my udders out and go for a walk, so I need to find Mummee and shouty bitch (ha! don't let on I called her that). Tiiiiiiittttccchhhhhh, where is Mummee, do you know? *Yes, she's in the garden, but I have no idea what she is doing, shall I go and annoy her?* NO, we just need to let her know I have to go pee. *Well do it in the garden, like you usually do.* I don't want to, and besides I need to stretch my legs, I have been sat for too long on Twitter, so go and shout at her.

She's coming! I kept putting my bally at her feet and barking - she got super annoyed, and is now coming inside, am I a genius or what?

ERM, no! She's here now - come on, let's wait by the front door, that usually does the trick.

Ha, we are out, and boy the freaks are in abundance today! Henry (fart breath) came waddling by, and Titch yelled, in German, "Stinkenden Penner" (stinky bum). The poor sod thought she was shouting hello, so shouted back, "Alright, my pals!" As we passed him I caught a whiff of his breath, and Jesus H Christ on a bike, it made my eyes water.

We also spotted Dummy Cat, sitting in his favourite spot, the window, looking suitably condescending. I wonder why he never comes out... maybe he is some kind of house cat, how awful though never breathing fresh air, but having said that, if he passed Henry, he would think we lived in a dumpster, ha.

Ha, Titch is on form again today - she has just spotted Klaus, also known as Frankfurter (as he resembles a sausage), and boy did she go to town on him. However, I failed to tell her that he is German also, so she is in trouble now, and there is a stand-off. Oops, I better go and intervene.

Come on, calm down, she didn't mean it, of course you are not a flat wanker! Titch, apologise to Klaus now! *Ggggrrrrr NO, he called me a kläffende Flohtasche!* Well, what's that? *A yapping flea bag, and I do not have fleas, ggggrrrrr, so he can sod off. Go and find yourself a bun to hide in, you idiot sausage dog, ha ha ha.* OMG, you have really upset him, look, his tail is tucked under... oh dear, this has gone from bad to wurst! Ha, we are like Laurel and Hardy, a great comedy duo.

Alright, alright, enough now, apologise, both of you, otherwise it will be a nightmare every time we pass each other. *OK, I am sorry, Klaus, I didn't mean to antagonise you and call you stupid names, let us call a truce.* Right now, that's sorted, shall we continue on, and see if we can get back home without further drama.

Back home now; however, as we passed Dummy Cat's house, Titch decided to run up to the window again. Mummee was annoyed as she said it was dangerous, she could have gotten run over, and also, frightening the cat like that was not funny. Titch and I however thought it was hilarious, the stupid cat fell for it again, and jumped six feet in the air, knocking the ornaments off the windowsill at the same time. His owners will be upset with him when they get home, ha ha!

Just gobbled down some nomtastic chicken-flavoured chew stick... Titch had never had one before and so was savouring hers... I tried to grab it off her but she bit me, and shouted, *"step away from my chewy stick you fatso froggy dog, it's mine, all mine, ggggrrrr"*. Alright, calm down, jeez.

So, I have sent the tweet out about it soon being Titch's birthday, and could all our wonderful followers please let me know what we can do to make it special, as she has never had a birthday before. My BF, Stuffy, has come back with a brilliant idea and said get in touch with Fitz again and ask him if he could actually meet up with Titch in a park, instead of just the Skype thingy. OMG Stuffy, you are awesome!

Messaged BC and wished her a happy day, and said wouldn't it be wonderful if we could meet? She came back with a resounding NO. I did ask her though if she could retweet the info for the auction and she has, and said I was a kind D.O.G. Well yes I am, in fact I have just checked the auction and so far it is up to £100, which is pawsome. A lovely lady in Florida has bid on the book, and hopes to win it. I shall check back later when the auction is finished to see.

Sent a message to Fitz, and explained that as Titch had never had a birthday, we had now decided to say it was 2nd July, and would he, as a huge surprise, be able to meet her in our local park? Now I just have to wait for his reply.

All of this organising has left me exhausted, I think I will just grab me forty winks, maybe even stretch it to fifty, and then I shall check back and see what responses I have received, so see ya -wouldn't want to be ya! ZZZZzzzzz

Fatso is snoring his head off, so I thought I would jump in on his blog and tell you another story. Don't worry, it's not a sad one this time, it happened when I was in the kennel with my great pal Fitz. I remember that it happened on a Saturday because that's when we always got to run in the yard, as we called it, a fenced-off area with lush green grass we could roll in.

Fitz and I were following our usual routine of lying close to the fence seeing if we could find a way to dig a hole to the other side. It never happened in all the time we were in there - the fence was imbedded too deep into the earth - but we used to dream of fields filled with families, each waiting for their new furry family member. This dream is what kept us going.

Anyway, I digress. There we were, scratching away at the earth, when Fitz stopped suddenly and said to me look, incoming! Well

when I looked up, I do not know how I didn't fall over with laughter. Trotting along, like some kind of show pony, was the campest, most idiotic-looking dog I ever laid eyes on. He/she (we didn't know until later it was a HE!) had fur balls on each of his ankles covering his paws, then NO fur on his legs, then his rear end was one giant pom-pom, then no more fur on his body until we got to his head and Jesus Holy Christ it was like a 70's Afro! I mean who the hell does this to a dog? No wonder the poor sod was being sent to concrete hell. Fitz and I simultaneously burst out laughing, and as you now know this sounds like barking, which in turn caused all the other dogs to stop what they were doing, and then it became a barking frenzy.

The poor sod didn't know what had hit him, he looked aghast, and stopped trotting and just stood stock still. But then he did the best thing ever, and each and every one of us howled, he started dancing on his hind legs!

We later learnt that his name was… wait for it… Pepper Prince! Well of course this caused more laughter amongst us all, but to be fair he was the kindest, sweetest dog, and his story was quite sad. He had been a show poodle, and used to compete in competitions, which is why his fur was shaved as it was, but, one day, he went to get his owner up, and found that she had died. He was left all alone, as there were no relatives to take him. He was devastated. He ended up at first in the vet's, but they couldn't keep him, and then he went to a foster family for a while, but they were having a baby and so couldn't keep him, and so that's why he came to the concrete place.

We took care of him and each night he would perform for us, doing his dancing act, it was great fun. Then one day a family came in and took one look at him and fell in love. By this time his fur had grown back so he no longer had the ridiculous pom-poms or Afro, and he looked more like a regular dog. We all barked our salute to him as he left, and for one last time he did the dance. What a great guy Pepper Prince was, we were all so happy he found his forever home, after his sad journey... and now that is it, I can hear Fatso rousing, so better scarper quick, you know how protective he can be of his blog!

Bloody hell, that was some snooze... I am sure I dreamed of BC and she was confessing her undying love for me, oh how that would be wonderful - she makes my little heart beat faster, and every time I see her eyes, I drool! HA, I better not let on about that last bit.

Oh FFS, Titch has been on here I see, what has she been blabbering away about now? Let's have a look, mmm, HA HA HA Pepper Prince, what kind of camp name is that? Wait until I tell BF - that is worse than Mr Chicken's stage name, Hen-Rietta, talking of which I need to find out what the score is with him.

Just tweeted BF and asked her about Mr Chicken. She said, didn't I remember that they agreed to be just friends, as he couldn't decide which team he played for? I was confused, I said I thought he came out of the closet ages ago, and I couldn't understand his upset at her over sailor cat. This whole thing doesn't make much sense. I think in future I shall leave her to make her own decisions.

Tweeted BC, and said her eyes reminded me of the ocean, deep and blue, and her neck rolls were so alluring. Oops, I don't think I should've mentioned her neck rolls, as she replied, well at least I can see my paws, Fatso. Touchy or what? I bet her Dad isn't this sensitive, especially with his quick wit - she needs to take a leaf out of his book.

Oh well, you win some, you lose some... talking of which, I wonder how my auction is doing... it finishes very soon, in fact in less than three minutes... This is exciting, it has only gone and reached £140, and the lady in Florida is the winner! This is fantastic, what a brilliant day, all I need now is to hear from Fitz and it will be the best day ever.

Well folks, joy of joys, I have had a message back from Fitz, and he has said that he could travel to our local park with his Mum next Saturday and meet up with me and Titch, which is absolutely fantastic as that is the 2nd July - the "birthday date" we agreed on. OMG, I cannot contain my excitement, what a great surprise this is going to be. I just have to organise the time and how we can get her there without her catching on, but that should be easy... Right - first thing is, message Fitz back.

Message: Hi Fitz, you don't know how happy this has made me, and my goodness when Titch sees you, her eyes will light up! I just know it will be the best "first" birthday for her; you are so kind. Do you think you could make it to the park for 10 am, before it gets too hot? Let me know if this is ok.

Rupert

Right, now that's done, time to tweet BC and let her know who won the auction, and tell her that my heart will always belong to her, and that even if she does have fifty-two other fiancés, none of them will ever be MOI!

Ha, she responded, saying well done for the auction, and as for me ever being her fiancé: NEVER, in capitals. Alright, alright, calm down, blimey. Let's see what the Twitter family has been up to – oooo, interesting, Viv is off to see the funny man in his own show. I'm a bit jealous, as I would love to meet him.

My bucket list, if you were interested (of course you are!) is as follows:

- Go to the beach (nope never been)
- Curl up on funny man's belly
- Help lots of poor animals by selling lots of books
- Eat ten chews in one sitting (nom nom)
- Go to New York and eat pizza with Stuffy
- Run through a field of strawberries (more nomm nomm)

And that is it, quite short I know, but my life is simple and I am not greedy, erm I hear laughter, fuck off! Let's see, what else is happening? Well, Vicki has bought a bee house, but it looks rather sad and depressing... if any bees move into that I shall eat my paw. It would be like staying in the Bates Motel, HA! You are probably wondering about my PA, well she has been busy editing my book, scanning for grammar and spelling mistakes. What a wonderful woman she is, I am honoured to have found her. If it wasn't for Twitter, I would have never had her in my life, so I am truly lucky. *Wow that's nice Rupert, I didn't have to put that in myself!* No problem PA – take the rest of the day off. Hmm, on second thought no, better wait till you have finished editing this chapter.

Twitter can be a great place, where like-minded hoomans and furry warriors come together, and I am especially lucky to have met such wonderful folks. All my followers are a great bunch, especially my BF Stuffy. Speaking of whom, I shall just send her a message... It looks like she is sleeping, so I left her a message for when she wakes up, saying I hope she didn't fall asleep with her stuffing on show. Ok that is enough Twittering - I shall go and see what madam is up to... oo hang on, before I go, I see I have a new message, and it's from Fitz, YES, he can do 10 am, brilliant.

Titch, where are you? *In here Fatso, just staring into space. I'm bored, what shall we do?* Come on, let's go and play in the garden, we can sniff out snails. *Cool, can we eat them?* YUK NO, in fact I think they can cause some kind of disease, so if you see any just nudge them, and then watch as they

disappear into their shells, it's like magic!
Come on, I'll show you.

*Hey Rupert, do you know if Fitz has messaged
me? He said he would, but when I last
checked nothing had come through... oh god,
what if he never contacts me again, what will I
do? I will be so upset, oh this is awful!*
FUCKING HELL, will you shut up, calm
down, don't forget he is a busy dog. He will be
in touch. Now come on, let's find the snails.

Hey, Rupe, look what I've found! What is it, is
it a mousey? Ooo it's a mousey, quick, catch
it! *IT'S NOT A MOUSEY, what is it with you
and mousey? You are obsessed. It's a snail
without a shell, look!* IDIOT – ouch! Why is it
when I call you an idiot you bite me, yet
when you call me one, that's ok? You have
such double standards. *Erm, I do not. Firstly,
I am by far more intelligent than you, and,
secondly, you are an idiot of epic proportions -
loving that cat for starters, when you know
she's never gonna love you back.* Yes well
alright, but the heart wants what the heart
wants, I am an old romantic... but back to
that thing, it is not a snail without a shell, it's

a worm. They do good things - help the soil, feed the birds - so leave him.

Alright you old fat romantic, come on now, let's go in. I'm a little sleepy - could do with a snooze, you want to join me? Is that just the dumbest question ever, do I want to join you? Like erm YEAH, come on.

That was some snooze, we both snuggled in comfy bed, and I must admit it was bliss. I really do love my sister now. She is my best pal, apart from Stuffy of course, who I see is awake now – I need to tell her the news about Fitz, and also see what other ideas our Twitter family has come up with.

Right, BF is awake, and said that she almost fell asleep in a cab the other day... she dozed off, but luckily woke up before it was too late, otherwise it could've been a catastrophe - she would've ended up in the Bronx, and that is somewhere she doesn't feel safe. I asked why, but she said she doesn't even want to talk about it. Crikey, must have been bad! Anyway, I quickly moved on to tell her about the surprise, with Fitz agreeing to meet Titch next week, and she cheered up immediately. It is just so brilliant! The only thing, I said, that would make it even greater would be if she could be there, but there's too much sea between us, maybe one day.

I also had some great suggestions from the Twitter family; they said how about they all send birthday messages on the day, with funny pics and videos to keep her entertained? I said fantastic. Even BC said she would sing Happy Birthday to her, which I thought was really kind. This is turning out to be the best birthday ever! Roll on next week...

Hey Fatso, whatcha doing? Let me see, ooo is that BC? What does she want? Nothing, keep your nose out ok, isn't it time for a walk anyway? Come on, I can hear Mummee calling us.

It's certainly a hot one today. We don't go out in the midday sun, so Mummee either takes us very early, or after 7 pm, and yet this evening it is still roasting, my udders have nearly melted into the pavement! Oh jeez, I hope we don't have to stay out much longer, this is unbearable. I really don't like the heat. I also suffer with allergies, so any kind of pollen makes me itchy; I take special tablets, which in turn make me fat.

Hey Titch, are you not hot? *Yes, I am actually, but I am used to it, as when I was in the concrete jungle with Fitz, we had a blinding hot summer and it was like being inside an oven. They had to order in special cold blowers to keep us all cool, and we had big bowls of water... They even put a massive swimming pool in the yard, and it was when Pepper Prince was still with us, oh that was hilarious - he jumped in it, and all his fur shrank up, he looked like a scouring pad, ha! So after living in that heat for all that time, I acclimatised I suppose, but it will be worse for you, what with being fat and all!* Hey, I've told you I can't help it, but yes, it's unpleasant.

I think we are heading back; even Mummee is sweating, and mumbling about how hot it is... oh look, there's Henry - whatever you do, don't say anything, and do not get too close to him. I bet in this heat his breath will be like that of a dragon who's eaten camel shit EWWWW.

Oi Henry, alright mate, why do you have flies swarming round you? Hahahaha! OMG, I told you not to say anything, you can't help yourself, can you? Well look at him now, looking all dazed and confused, looking for flies. You idiot. Ouch! Right, let us just get home, I need water, and to lie on the cold tiles. I have to cool my udders down before they burn and explode like a bottle of propane.

Thank Christ we are back, what a sticky night! Well, may as well see what's what in the Twitterverse, and let everyone know that we will be out at 10 am on Saturday, so they should tweet their birthday wishes to Titch either early in the morning or after.

Just tweeted BC, and told her that if she were my fiancée I would take her to the moon and back, she answered with NO THANK

YOU BUZZ FATSO! I must admit even I think that is funny. Oh I also tweeted some of my philosophy, as my thoughts can be quite deep at times... I said the early bird gets the worm, but the second mouse gets the cheese! I am a genius disguised as a dog... well that's enough fun today on Twitter, time for a snooze, not long now until the surprise.

WAKE UP, WAKE UP, WAKE UP, IT IS YOUR BIRTHDAY!!! Whooooooo hoooooo, and have I got a surprise for you, we are going to duck bastard park with Mummee!

OMG, It's my birthday for real, you will call me by my full regal name today, Princess Consuela Bananarama Ninny Nanny Noo Noo, and you will do as I say ALL DAY. This is the best day ever, and I have even had loads of tweets already from our followers, wishing me a very special day... also you will never guess what, BC tweeted me and meowed Happy Birthday to me! That is totally amazing... OK, when are we going to duck bastard park?

We will go to the park just as soon as
Mummee has had breakfast, and given Dad
his - he likes to have a "full English" on
Saturdays, whatever that is! All I know is the
smell drives me crazy, and it looks like he
has yummy stuff on his plate, but he eats it
at the table, so I can only ever see the edge of
the plate, and I am not allowed any of it!
HEY, maybe you will have better luck, and
what with you being more agile, perhaps try
jumping on one of the chairs to take a peek.
Come on, let's go and see.

*OOOO Rupert, shame you are a fatso, as the
view from up here is incredible! Dad has on
his plate mushrooms, eggs, tomatoes,
sausage, some funny-looking orange things,
and toast, it is making my mouth water! I
wonder if he will give me any, I am going to
give him my best sad doe-eyed look, and if he
does give in, I shall share it with you, ok?* Oh
god, do it, I would love some sausage, nom
nom, I am salivating just thinking about it.

*HA, in your face Fatso, this is the best
goddam sausage I have ever tasted, shame
Dad didn't give you any... I tried, I really did!*

That is evil, you promised you would share, not run off with it! I cannot believe you have done this to me, what with the surprise... *Did you just say surprise, oo what is it? I thought duck bastard park was the surprise, OMG, are we going to get to eat a duck?* NOOOOO you are a fucking maniac, we are not going to eat a duck, FFS. Wait and see, then you will be saying sorry to me for not sharing that sausage.

Right, we are nearly there, are you ok? *Yes, just about, the car ride wasn't as bad as I thought, and because we could see out of the window I didn't actually feel sick... Wow look at the size of duck bastard park, bloody hell, we better not get lost in here!* No fear of that with Mummee, she doesn't let us off these leads, that's why they extend out so we can roam, but not get lost, good eh? So, I just have to wander off a minute - you stay by Mummee, I shall be just by that tree over there... *Over where?* That one there with that dog by it... *Which one? oh yeah... OH MY FUCKING GOD, is that who I think it is? It's Fitz, is it him, really, how the hell is he in the same park as us, on my birthday as well? This is insane, Rupert, can you believe this?*

DUH, well I wonder how this happened, possibly this is the surprise! Come on, keep up.

ARRRGGHH I'm going to cry, this is the best goddam fricking amazing most awesome day ever. What a fan-bloody-tastic birthday surprise, you are really the kindest, most wonderful brother ever! I am sorry I stole the sausage - I will make it up to you I promise - but for now, I have to get over there to Fitz! FIIITTZZZ, FIIITTTZZZZ, it's me, Titch, I'm coming.

Fitz, this is incredible, I cannot believe you are here in the fur, and my, you look so well and handsome, come here and let me sniff you! Hey Titch, it is so wonderful to see you, little one, you look so happy and well yourself, it pleases me to see you with this forever family! I take it they treat you with kindness? *Oh yes, they are the best, and here is my new brother Fatso, oops sorry Rupert... come on Rupes, say hi to Fitz.*

Hi Fitz, great to finally meet you! You hold a special place in her heart, and this means so much to her, I can see it on her face. Thank you for coming out of your way, the journey must have been tough.

It was, Rupert, but all worth it, and Titch is always in my heart. I can't tell you how much it means to me seeing her settled and happy. For a long time when she first came to the concrete jungle, she was very sad and frightened. With what that bastard did to her, he wants tearing apart.

Yes, she told me the story, but I get the impression she left some of it out, as it was too painful, but I'm with you on that Fitz - if I ever had the misfortune to meet him, I would bite his bollocks off. Anyway, this is a happy day, and I know you cannot stay long, so why not have a wander over to the trees in the shade and have a catch up? I am off to annoy the duck bastards, ha.

Fitz, seeing you after all this time is like a dream, I never ever thought our paths would cross again, and yet here you are! This day has been so overwhelming, and it was all arranged by that fat little idiot over there. He has totally surprised me with this kindness and warm heart, almost as big as yours Fitz.

Hey, don't cry, come on now, this is a happy day, and I would say that fat idiot of yours has a heart as big as mine, he sure does love you. I feel content now Titch, knowing you are in a happy place, and you are with a kind family. I can cross it off my list.

What list, what are you on about? My bucket list, it's a list of things I want to do before I have to say goodbye. *Erm, you have only just got here, dope, and what kind of stupid name is a bucket list? I have no idea what you are wittering on about. Come on, let's go and bark at the ducks!* Yeah, come on little one, let's have some fun, it looks like Rupert is already ahead of us, HA.

Rupert, this day has been THE MOST astounding day ever, I just don't know how you are going to top that next year! Maybe Fitz can come and visit us where we live? Let's see ok, but for now we need to be getting back, did you say goodbye to Fitz? *I did, yes, but he was blabbering on about some bucket list, I have no idea what he was on about, do you?* Oh that, no, nothing for you to worry about, especially on this day, and what a day. Happy birthday, sister.

Hey everyone [*whispering], in the last message I had from Fitz, he said that he would be honoured to come and meet Titch for one last time, in fact it was on his bucket list, funnily enough. He also confided in me that his last trip to the vet wasn't good, they thought he perhaps only had a few weeks left with us on this earth, but he asked me to please not say anything to Titch to spoil her special day.

So, folks, the brave and splendid Fitz will soon be OTRB, which in our animal world means over the rainbow bridge, where our souls go and we live on. It saddens me to break this to you, as he was a mighty fine dog. His legs are weak, he said, and his heart is failing, but the love he has for Titch will never die, and he was so glad to have seen her one last time, happy and free.

The End

Or is
it...
....

No animals, or hoomans were hurt in the writing of this book, all names changed to protect the innocent, accept for Viv who is far from innocent and one of the funniest ladies I know, also Vicki she is real too, oh and BC, short for Beauty Cat, real name Ollie my friend, oh and Stuffy, my BF.

36357326R00106

Printed in Poland
by Amazon Fulfillment
Poland Sp. z o.o., Wrocław